"You should know better than anyone that I won't play your games again, *shahzadi*. Fool me once, and all that."

"It's not a game. More of a social media masquerade. A temporary fake relationship to titillate my fans and the media, to satisfy Zia's fiancé's family that I'm a lovesick traditional woman after all. A stay order for all the destruction that powerful minister is raring to rain on you. I've even picked out the hashtag to defeat all hashtags. And if you're going to be all macho man about it," she said with a forced laugh, "I'll be the prey and you can play the predator."

Virat's light brown eyes gleamed in the flickering lights. "Is this some kind of new kink you discovered? Because if it is, *shahzadi*, all you have to do is tell me. I'd be more than happy to play the master."

Zara flushed, tiny pinpricks of desire shooting all over her skin. It shocked her how much she wanted to say yes. How much she wanted to feel his mouth on hers. How much she wanted to play whatever role he wanted her to as long as it ended up with her being underneath him.

Born into Bollywood

Legends in the limelight meet their match!

Vikram and Virat Raawal are the uncrowned kings of Bollywood. Born into an influential family that has ruled the Bollywood industry for generations, the time has come for the spotlight to fall firmly on their legacy!

As the world around them glitters, the golden boys of Bollywood hide a family of scandal and deceit. But they are about to discover that once in a lifetime there is someone who can turn their world upside down and cut through the superstardom to the men behind the masks!

A masked ball and a one-night stand is about to set Vikram's world on fire in *Claiming His Bollywood Cinderella.*

Virat will be signing up for much more than a fake romance when he's reunited with an old flame in *The Surprise Bollywood Baby.*

Both available now!

Tara Pammi

THE SURPRISE BOLLYWOOD BABY

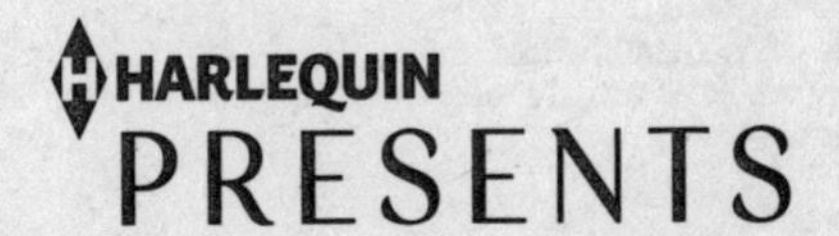

Recycling programs for this product may not exist in your area.

ISBN-13: 978-1-335-40390-2

The Surprise Bollywood Baby

This edition published by arrangement with Harlequin Books S.A.

For questions and comments about the quality of this book, please contact us at CustomerService@Harlequin.com.

Harlequin Enterprises ULC
22 Adelaide St. West, 40th Floor
Toronto, Ontario M5H 4E3, Canada
www.Harlequin.com

Printed in U.S.A.

Tara Pammi can't remember a moment when she wasn't lost in a book—especially a romance, which was much more exciting than a mathematics textbook at school. Years later, Tara's wild imagination and love for the written word revealed what she really wanted to do. Now she pairs alpha males who think they know everything with strong women who knock that theory and them off their feet!

Books by Tara Pammi

Harlequin Presents

Born into Bollywood

Claiming His Bollywood Cinderella

Conveniently Wed!

Sicilian's Bride for a Price

Once Upon a Temptation

The Flaw in His Marriage Plan

The Scandalous Brunetti Brothers

An Innocent to Tame the Italian
A Deal to Carry the Italian's Heir

Visit the Author Profile page
at Harlequin.com for more titles.

To all the readers who have picked up a book of mine—thank you! This journey wouldn't be possible without you.

CHAPTER ONE

After a decade-long affair, Bollywood Queen Zara Khan is dumped by Vikram Raawal for a younger model!

"Nobody Naina" steals boss Zara Khan's man right from under her nose!

Vikram Raawal's massive biopic set to sink even before release!

ZARA KHAN LOOKED at the headlines on three different websites in dawning horror and put away her cell phone. She stole a quick glance at her assistant, Naina, also her longtime best friend Vikram Raawal's fiancée. Her signature curls framing her small face, Naina sat at the back table with Vikram's sister, Anya. Even from this distance, Zara could see the strain on Naina's face.

Had Naina already seen these? Was that the reason for how subdued she'd been for the past week—this ridiculous suggestion that somehow she'd stolen

Vikram away from Zara? That she'd destroyed Zara's chance at happiness?

Where and how did the media come up with these disgusting lies?

This was the last thing the happy couple needed, just a week before their wedding—Zara's rabid fan base to send ill wishes their way. After standing by Zara through thick and thin, after a lifetime spent righting the mighty ship of his family's rocky finances and reputation and that of the Raawal House of Cinema, Vikram deserved to have his and Naina's happiness unmarred by all this drama and dirt.

Even though she had already made a public statement about how happy she was for Vikram and Naina, it hadn't made a speck of difference to her legion of fans.

And it wasn't limited to silly rumors, either, that she wished all of them could simply weather until something more salacious hit the news cycle.

This gossip about Vikram's supposed breakup with Zara and his simultaneous engagement to Naina was becoming the defining narrative around the upcoming biopic telling the story of how Vikram's grandfather, Vijay Raawal, had been inspired to create his production house. Every interview Vikram had tried to give about the project had been hijacked by the media to ask him about his relationship struggles.

Frustration filled her muscles and Zara struggled to keep her expression smiling and graceful as the program for the launch of the lifestyle website *SuperWomen*, which Zara was one of the prime investors for, continued on stage.

If she hadn't promised the group of smart young women who had created the website that she would throw her weight and name behind the launch, and if she hadn't already spent the considerable goodwill she had in the industry to wrangle powerful men into attending it, Zara would have walked out of the event. The last thing she wanted to do right now was to be her graceful self on stage while every man and woman watching wondered if she was secretly nursing a broken heart.

Damn it, no one was going to reduce her to the role of victim. She hadn't done that even when she had just cause to. She certainly wasn't going to begin now.

It was time to take action. The last thing Vikram needed this close to his wedding to Naina was this much bad publicity.

With the biopic in full production already and slated to be finished within the next few weeks, this much bad sentiment toward Vikram had real consequences, especially as he'd sunk everything he had into the project. It was time to give the media a new distraction. Time to give her fan base something even more delicious and exciting to speculate about than Vikram and Naina's engagement. Time to bring the focus back to the biopic, where it belonged.

A niggle of a plan began to hatch at the back of Zara's mind the moment she saw Virat Raawal walk in from the foyer, all casual grace and swaggering masculinity. Heads turned toward him and whispers abounded as they always did whenever he appeared.

While Vikram was traditionally handsome and had established himself as the uncrowned king of the acting industry through various carefully designed blockbusters, his brother, Virat, stood at the top of the directing hierarchy in a way no one could even compete with. Known for his brilliant storytelling across a number of internationally acclaimed movies, Virat was a true rebel in every way that mattered. Actors and actresses vied with each other to star in his movies, while writers created stories for him to bring to life on the silver screen.

With a patrician nose and rugged features, *beautiful* or *handsome* were words too…simple to describe the brilliant director. *Untamed* was the only word that came to Zara's mind every time she saw him. A man who wouldn't be caught by the simple constraints of a relationship or the boundaries by which everyone else lived.

A shiver of awareness gripped Zara—as familiar to her when he was anywhere in the vicinity as her own reflection. His tall, lean frame rounded the banquet hall, radiating an intensity that belied the cocky smile on his lips.

Zara always had the feeling he was laughing at the world, instead of with it. With pure contempt. As if they were all insignificant pawns in a game only he knew how to play.

While every man here—most of them pioneers in their industry—was dressed to the nines in three-piece suits, Virat of course flouted the dress code in a fitted white shirt and black trousers that molded to his six-foot-two-inch frame. His pristine shirt, three buttons undone, formed a deliciously contrasting V against his dark skin.

Ten years ago, at just twenty years old, he'd been full of an innate confidence and wicked charm that Zara hadn't been able to resist. Now he wore his power as comfortably and as effortlessly as his custom-made shirts.

The shadow of a beard and a cigar hanging from the edge of his full mouth completed the picture of the disreputable genius, as the world called him. With him looking like that, the recent news of his dangerous affair with a powerful cabinet minister's young wife was all too easy to believe.

Apparently, the man lived his life the way he made his movies—skating the edge of propriety, pushing the boundaries of society, with a hefty dose of mockery and contempt. No one had missed the showdown the minister had tried to force on Virat not a week ago. No one in the industry could be oblivious to the rumors that the minister was using every ounce of his reach to hurt Virat where it would do the most damage.

Zara sent a silent thanks to the universe that at least he hadn't shown up at this launch with the minister's young wife in tow. She had wondered if he would even show up at all.

But now that he was here, she didn't have a moment to lose to execute her plan. If she thought about it too much, if she pondered on what she was putting into motion with the man who hated her very guts, the one man who'd always be her weakness, then she would talk herself out of it.

She would run far away.

Instead Zara stood up from her seat and dragged in a few deep breaths under the guise of straightening her white silk shirt and emerald green skirt. Her knees wobbled as she made her way toward the group of men that were laughing uproariously at whatever brilliant piece of wit Virat had bestowed on them.

Once, Zara hadn't been his equal. She had walked out of his life because she hadn't trusted herself to be good enough for him.

Now, at least when measured by the world's superficial and arbitrary definition of success, Zara Khan—sometimes dubbed Bollywood Queen for her continued and sustained success at the age of thirty-five in an industry that swapped veteran actresses for the latest young thing like they were yesterday's leftovers, was more than good enough to take on Virat Raawal.

If it meant giving Naina and Vikram a better start to their life together, if it meant saving all their asses with regards to the biopic, Zara would do anything. Even if it meant tangling with the reckless playboy who hated her very guts, who would take every opportunity to use what she was giving him to torment her for God only knew what sins.

She was up to something.

Zara Khan, actress extraordinaire and astute businesswoman, should be firmly embedded in his distant past but kept shimmering like an enticing beacon in his present. No, strike that. She was more like a niggling thorn lodged in his skin.

And damn it all to hell, but Virat Raawal felt every inch of him practically vibrating with an anticipation and excitement he hadn't tasted in a long time. He ran a hand through his hair, cursing his tunnel focus on his current project for the last eighteen months.

From the moment he had stepped into the banquet hall and found her watching him with undisguised attention, Virat had known something was afoot. Tracking his every move from that wide-eyed gaze. Making his skin prickle with awareness.

She couldn't have been more obvious if she'd thrown herself at him—all grace and curves and self-confidence oozing out of every inch of flawless skin she revealed.

No wonder his long-denied libido was now wagging its tail like an excited puppy at the sight of a much-coveted fancy treat.

Because that was what Zara was to him. A delicious treat that made him act like a man barely out of his teens, riding the roller coaster of horniness and emotional turbulence all over again.

Even after all these years. Even after he'd reminded himself countless times that she'd made her choice a long time ago. That she'd left no doubt as to whom she preferred, between the famous Vikram Raawal—the uncrowned king of Bollywood who'd slogged night and day for years, to save his family and the prestigious Raawal House of Cinema from dire straits—or him, Virat Raawal, the man whose questionable paternity was always a fan-favorite topic of conversation on the weekly chai-and-chat shows.

In the decade since she'd used him to climb up the ladder of success, Virat had built up a reputation both within the industry and with the critics—a reputation that his grandfather and cinema visionary Vijay Raawal had garnered more than half a century ago. A reputation and a body of work that had every artist in the industry salivating to work with him.

Even though they'd regularly butted heads on the direction of the family's production house, Virat had always had Vikram's support. The brothers' bond had been borne out of their parents' incapability to provide them with a modicum of emotional and mental stability in their lives. So Virat had actively worked on not letting the bitterness of Zara's choice or her long-standing relationship with his brother rot the bond between himself and Vikram. And he'd succeeded for the most part.

While he'd never understood their relationship, he'd left it alone. And now, with his brother about to marry the lovely Naina and the resulting nasty rumors about Vikram breaking Zara's heart, Virat had been thinking a lot more about their purported, decade-long relationship.

Tucking his hands into his trouser pockets, he absently nodded at some comment on his left when the subtle hint of Zara's scent hit his nostrils. Virat stiffened, as if bracing himself against an oncoming attack. He didn't have to turn and look at her to know that she had sidled up to him, closer than a woman he hardly ever talked to in ten years should have done.

Her bare arm rubbed up against his, the warmth of her curvaceous body a teasing caress. Virat scowled and was about to ask her what the hell she was up to when the roaming strobe light focused on them both and a cheer went up around the hall.

An announcement flashed on the huge screen propped at the top corner next to the stage just as a short, bespectacled woman announced his and Zara's names together as the primary investors in the web mag, calling out giveaways including and not limited to scholarships for female junior college students, a featured monthly charity drive for innovative small businesses from around the country's rural villages, and an opportunity for the chosen SuperWoman of the month to meet Zara and Virat. As their schedules allowed, of course.

"Shall we, darling?" Zara said then, loosely linking her arm through his, in that husky voice of hers that he could recognize in his sleep.

He turned his head to look at her then, beyond stunned. And Virat knew that everyone in the hall was watching them, with the same wide-eyed fascination that Zara was faking as she looked at him.

As if he was the answer to all her dreams and wishes.

Their gazes met and the world around them seemed to stand still. With her silky hair in a soft cut framing her sharp-angled face, Zara was the consummate actress. Her eyes shone with some inner resolve he couldn't read and the smile she offered him was wide and not in the least bit awkward. The lush lower lip painted a soft pink taunted him.

With her palm pressed to his chest, she winked at him and pouted. His blood pressure went up another notch, shock and desire twining into an inseparable rope. "I know you don't like PDAs, sweetie, but you promised to do this with me, remember?" Her thigh bumped against his when she leaned closer and it was a miracle that he didn't jump away like a scalded cat. Or more like an outraged heroine fending off the caricature villain in one of his brother's latest box-office hits.

He noted the flare of awareness in her eyes before she pulled back. Reaching for her waist, Virat twirled her out of earshot of the rest of the group, keeping his own expression mildly amused. She came as easily as if she were floating on air, her face barely betraying her shock. He pushed her against the far wall, and the circle of light followed them.

"Now what the hell are you playing at, *shahzadi*?" he whispered, while she clasped her hands at the nape of his neck. The slide of her soft fingers there sent tension and desire rolling through him in fast waves.

Her breath was a silky caress against his jaw as she whispered, "It's all for a good cause, Virat. Play along, won't you?"

"Play along as what? Your latest boy toy?"

She laughed and shrugged. "Something like that, yes."

The warm, husky sound wrapped around his

heart like a tight fist, rushing in vivid memories he'd buried deep for ten long years. There had always been something sensuous and magical about Zara's ability to laugh. Both at the world and at herself. Her sheer verve for life.

Was he the only one to be so besieged by those memories? Still so haunted? Was she so completely unaffected?

Their legs tangled all the way now, but she didn't back down. The slight tremble she tried to hide gave him a sudden stab of savage satisfaction. "I would love to, Zara. Even though playing games is your forte, not mine." He tucked a strand of silky hair that had fallen forward back behind her ear and she hissed in a breath. Yes, two could play these games apparently. But whatever it was, this time, he would win. Not come second to his older brother. "But I like the rules to be clear and upfront before I play with any woman, *shahzadi*. I have standards that have to be met. Even with repeat participants like yourself who want another round on the roller coaster."

"That's an awful thing to say about me. And yourself," she said, planting those long nails on his arm, her lovely smile out in full force.

"But accurate, yes?"

She sighed and nodded. "You're mistaking my intent here."

"Am I? Do you want me to pretend that we're innocents who don't know how the game is played?"

She glared at him, a glittering intensity to her brown eyes. But the damned woman didn't back down. Of course, she didn't. Despite everything she had done to get to where she was now, Virat couldn't help but admire her sheer tenacity in forging the glittering career she'd always wanted, and for sustaining it for so long.

In four-inch heels, she made up the difference between their heights. When she leaned closer still, her luscious, pink mouth reached his ear. Virat had to fight down a shiver. Gilded by long eyelashes, her eyes held his with a stubborn resolve. "Fine, then. Believe me when I say that this is a much-needed distraction. One small farce to be played out so that…"

Those expressive eyes flicked to someone in the back. Virat followed her gaze and found his on Naina, his soon-to-be sister-in-law, who was trying to downplay her curiosity at Zara's sudden public display. And with him, of all men.

But what he didn't miss was the sudden surge of curious whispers that already filled the hall, like the drone of bees.

"So that what?" he prompted, having already noted the dark circles under Naina's eyes when he'd met her earlier in the day. Caught up as he'd been in his own work, he still hadn't been oblivious to all the nightmarish, nasty rumors swirling around his brother and his fiancée. With Zara at the center of it all, being portrayed as the poor rejected ex-lover.

Zara noted his impatience. "So that other genuinely deserving people like Naina and Vikram can be given a respite from all the drama. So that you can save your own backside from the powerful minister's reach. So that we can both stop Vikram's biopic from sinking before it even gets released."

For a few seconds there, he'd wondered if Zara had started all the rumors to make herself look better in the world's press. But Virat couldn't discount the genuine quality of her friendship with his brother or the generosity with which she had taken Naina under her wing.

He had no idea what she saw in his eyes but she sighed and said, "Oh, for God's sake, Virat, don't look at me like that. You can't be surprised that I know of the troubles you're having thanks to your affair with the minister's young wife. Or that the biopic has been mired in one trouble after another ever since production began."

"I'm not surprised that you have your finger on the pulse of it all, as usual," he countered, as hundreds of eyes stared at the spectacle unfolding right in front of them. As much as he hated it, he couldn't discount the genius of her idea. Of how close he was to wrapping up everything he needed for the documentary series he was secretly filming, and how much he didn't need the extra scrutiny from the powerful and corrupt cabinet minister he was about to expose. "Or that you have contacts in high places and know how to use them."

She blinked and he had a feeling he'd hurt her with that last comment. But he'd learned his lesson the hard way to never trust Zara. To never believe the bright, intelligent eyes, or the flashes of vulnerability that had once fascinated him. Even now apparently. "So what is your concern, then?" she asked, a bite to her tone.

"For myself, of course," he added, his blood buzzing on a new high already. There was nothing more addictive than going toe to toe with this woman. Mere words bandied with her had more effect on his libido than rolling around naked with any other woman he'd known. He traced the line of her jaw, wrestling with his own hunger. "I don't know that I'm up to playing the role of your willing slave again, *shahzadi.* I don't know that I'm strong enough to survive it."

She gasped and swatted him. And he had a feeling that at least a hundred cameras were recording them right now. Of course, that was why she'd made her move at this launch party. Where she was already playing the central role. "It's not like I mean to swallow you and spit you out. You're not some innocent prey caught in the claws of some hungry female predator."

He raised a brow, a smile tugging at his lips. "Those are your words, Zara. Not mine."

"So?"

"So what?"

"So will you play along and pretend we're together?"

"For now, yes. Not that you have left me much of a choice."

He flicked his finger at the tip of her nose, refusing to give weight to the flash of hurt in her face.

"Let's finish what you started. Then you and I will walk out of here and have a long talk."

"Long talk about what?" Uncertainty filled her voice for the first time this evening.

"You sound scared, Zara."

"Of course I'm not scared of you. I ambushed you tonight, didn't I?"

"Ah…of course. The cryptic message I got about a source if I came here tonight was from you."

She shrugged. "You left me no choice. I had Naina call your assistant three times in the last week since I returned from my shoot. You were incommunicado."

"I was busy."

"With the minister's young wife, of course."

"Beginning to feel jealous of younger women like the papers are hinting at, are you?"

"Of course I'm not. You should know that everything they're writing about this strangely perverted love triangle between Naina, Vikram and me is… utter rubbish at best. Disgusting drivel at worst. Also remember that while I can shove it under the rug and rise above it, your soon-to-be sister-in-law can't. This has cast such an awful pall over Naina. I'd hate for it to cause more problems at the wedding or for their life together to begin on such a sour note."

The worry in her tone forestalled his instinctive response. "We will talk about terms and conditions for this new game, then. So that we can ensure both of us get what we desperately want out of this new… adventure."

"I want nothing from you," she retorted defensively and then blushed. Protesting much?

"One evening in my company and you might be ready to revise that declaration, Zara. In fact, if I remember right, there was one particularly delightful evening ten years ago when we were supposed to sneak into one of Vikram's launch parties so that he would notice you and instead we—"

Her palm landed on his mouth and their gazes held. An electric current arced between them, every bit as powerful and intense as it had been ten years ago. "If you think I've forgotten even one second of the things we did, then you have me all wrong, Virat. But this…this is about something more than you and me.

"Something that's bigger than our petty differences and ego wars."

"Petty differences, *shahzadi*? We will see about that."

Virat wrapped his fingers around her wrist and gently pulled her away from the wall. Her skin was so utterly soft against his calloused hands. "Lead the way," he said, finally breaking eye contact and releasing a long breath.

She nodded and they turned toward the stage as one.

He didn't remove his arm from around her waist and she didn't put any distance between their brushing bodies. They walked down the red carpet to the dais, their strides in rhythm as if they'd done this a thousand times before. As if they shared an intimacy that the world knew nothing about.

As if they knew each other inside out, better than anyone else.

A long time ago, he'd foolishly assumed that they did. With one move, Zara had proved to him that he didn't know her at all. That she wasn't the woman he'd thought her. And yet, this evening, something new had already begun. Something that was beyond both of them. Something that his entire body was primed for.

Zara and he had circled each other for ten years in the same industry, never coming too close. Never working on a project together, until with the biopic now. Never engaging with each other. There had been nothing to say or do while rumors of her continued entanglement with his brother abounded.

Now this, a fake romance, and the next few weeks of being together on the set of the biopic filming the final scenes meant the past was surely going to repeat itself.

He hadn't missed the flicker of interest she'd fought to hide from her eyes. He didn't lie to himself over his own interest in her. But this time, he reassured himself as they climbed the steps to the stage amid roaring applause, the ending of their relationship would be different. This time, he would make sure he was the one that walked away.

CHAPTER TWO

THE EVENING TURNED out to be a fantastic success—in terms of getting the man with a notorious reputation for not playing by the rules to cooperate with her and agree to behave as Zara's man of the hour.

As the evening came to an end, Zara signaled to Naina that she was free to leave. The last thing she wanted was to appease the curiosity shining in Naina's eyes when she and Virat still had to discuss "terms and conditions," as he'd put it. When the media was out in full force, hungry for the details of what they had teased out tonight.

Now it was time for their own personal showdown, to find out what the devil would demand as his due. Zara braced herself for it. She wasn't naive enough to think Virat's compliance as her boy toy for the near future would come without a very high price…

Her clutch in hand, Zara walked through the coffee lounge hidden behind a colorful, paneled wall on the hotel's ground floor. The pub was a well-kept secret, especially when one wanted to hide from the media.

Dark marble floor, handcrafted accents and clusters of low lighting gave the bar a retro, fun atmosphere. Virat sat at one of the high barstools around a table in a dimly lit corner. His discarded jacket was draped on the other barstool, his shirt still casually unbuttoned, a glass of Old Monk rum in a tumbler by his hand. His hair, piled high in a stylish haircut to accentuate those blade-like cheekbones, was mussed up.

As always, he had a tablet in front of him that he studied with that laser focus of his. Even in the quiet atmosphere of the bar, his restless energy dominated the space.

"Are you going to stand there and watch me all night, *shahzadi*?" came his deep voice in a husky murmur, his head still bent over the screen in front of him.

The endearment hit Zara low in the belly, and then moved up through her body, lodging painfully in her chest. Once upon a time, she'd loved it when he'd teased her like that. And if she was honest, there was a part of her that still liked it. A bit too much.

Except there wasn't that sweet indulgence in his voice anymore, and she wasn't a naive, gauche girl with stars in her eyes.

"Come closer. I won't bite. Unless you want me to."

Zara remained still, letting the longing pass through her. She'd had enough practice, having watched him afar for more than a decade. Having watched him go through woman after woman. He'd earned the reputation of being a brilliant director and an utter womanizer, both justly deserved.

"That endearment didn't make sense ten years ago," she said, covering the distance between them. "Given my lowly background, I've always been the farthest thing from a princess."

He still didn't look up when she arrived at the table, and the casual arrogance in the gesture stole her breath. "I'm used to thinking of you as a princess in training, *shahzadi*. Bad habits, as you know, are hard to shake."

"Was I a bad habit, then?" she fired back, before she could curb the self-indulgence. At least she sounded challenging, full of that verve she portrayed on-screen. At least she hadn't betrayed how much his opinion of her still mattered.

"Oh, the worst kind, *shahzadi*," he said, finally looking up. Cool brown eyes held hers, full of mockery and something more. Only a second's attention on her, then he flipped over another page on the device with his finger. "If one isn't careful, one could slide headlong back in…again and again."

Whether he meant to let her feel the heat in his words or not didn't matter. Zara felt memories sliding into the present, claiming her senses, lodging inside her muscles. God, he'd been such an incredible lover. And it shouldn't surprise her that within minutes of standing this close to him for the first time in a decade, her good sense wanted to fly away.

She waited for her heart to resume its normal pace. Tried to tell her swooping belly that the man was an incurable flirt. She bent her head and clicked the tiny button on his tablet closed. The screen turned black. "Ah…so you were telling the truth when you said you had to protect yourself from me? You're afraid of what I might do to you."

A smile curving his mouth, Virat leaned back into the seat. He rubbed a hand over his jaw, considering her. With one long leg, he pushed out a barstool for her to perch on. If Zara thought he might sputter at her innuendo, she'd have been wrong. This was not the Virat she'd known ten years ago—so full of raw emotions and intensity that it had been like looking at the sun. A man eager to prove himself to the world. Determined to leave the dirty rumors of his paternity behind.

This was a man who'd built and tasted success beyond his own wildest dreams. A man who lived his life by his own damned rules and no one else's.

"Is that why you picked me for this role, Zara? Because you think you can play me however you want?"

Zara snorted. "No, I picked you because this farcical affair will help you, too. And because I believe that, despite your differences, you do care about your brother."

A cold reserve entered his eyes. "So this is all about Bhai, then?"

Zara frowned. "It's not just Vikram that needs my help right now."

"I don't need you to save me, *shahzadi*."

"From the world? No. From yourself, yes," Zara retorted. "You were kind to me when I was at the worst point in my life. Let's just say I'm finally returning the favor. Maybe even taking the burden of talking some good sense into you off Vikram's shoulders."

"I forget how good you are at calculating your pros and cons. How risk averse you are. No wonder you and Bhai got along so well for so many years."

Zara stared at the clear contempt in his statement. That Virat and Vikram had always had differences in their vision for Raawal House of Cinema was publicly known. But to say *she* was calculating was...unfair. She wasn't calculating so much as she was risk averse. In both her career and in her personal life.

Especially when it came to men. Because she'd learned the hard way to be calculating. To deal with her head and not her heart.

Did Virat really believe the myriad rumors about her and Vikram's on-off relationship that was purported to have lasted throughout an entire decade? Did he think she'd simply traded one brother for the other when the fancy took her?

The very thought made her sick and angry. No, to think Virat was still affected in any way by the past was nothing but self-indulgence.

Virat Raawal attracted women like honey attracted bees. Maybe because he was such a generous lover. Maybe because he didn't play ego games like other men. Maybe because when he put his mind to it, he could be the kindest, funniest man a woman would ever meet.

He enjoyed the women who came to him and everything they offered. He gave them everything but his heart.

In the last ten years, he'd been through countless women, and she was a fool if she believed he'd been hung up on her even for a few days.

She shook her head, refusing to let the past cloud the present. "The point is, this situation you've created with your crazy antics with that minister's wife is bigger than both of us. Vikram's spent over fifteen years building up Raawal House of Cinema again, and he's finally found some measure of happiness with Naina. He's poured his heart and soul into this biopic, put everything he owns on the line. You're out of control, and if someone doesn't stop you, you'll bring everything down."

Virat's mouth tightened. "If I've become such a big liability because of my recent actions, then Bhai will simply fire me and find a new director. Like you, he's not sentimental."

"I don't think Vikram will fire you. Not when the production's more than half done. Not when this project already has your brilliant stamp all over it. This biopic is not any average project that you two have butted heads over. This is about your grandfather. This is Raawal House's magnum opus. This is a legacy that you and he will leave for generations to come..."

Zara softened her voice, knowing how long and how deep that old wound festered within him.

Virat Raawal's paternity had been fuel for speculation in countless magazine articles for over two decades. It was the alleged reason for his parents' scandalous second split, the reason for the huge chasm between his father and him, and it had been a painfully humiliating thorn in Virat's side from a young age.

Because his mother—the famous Bollywood star of yesteryear Vandana Raawal—had had a secret lover after her first split with her husband. Then had come their publicized reunion and mere months later, Virat had been born.

For most of his life, Virat had had to contend with exposés and articles and trashy interviews speculating about his paternity. With his father's cold rejection of him.

"Are you okay with being thrown out of that legacy, Virat?" Zara asked softly. "Have you decided that you don't want to be a Raawal after all?"

He ran his hand through his hair and groaned. "Enough with the regurgitation of the same sentimental rubbish, *shahzadi*. Mama's already put me through that speech, using the grand Raawal name to corral me." He looked up, his eyes shining with unholy mirth. "Of course, what you're offering as an incentive to behave is…clever."

"I'm not offering you anything," Zara blurted

out, like a green girl afraid of the slick charm in his words.

The rascal grinned, having successfully baited her. "So you trust me to behave as you want, then?"

Zara refused to let him play mind games with her. Even though her pulse raced with his every word, smile and touch. "What's there to not trust? You need to distract the minister's attention away from you. Vikram and Naina need to begin their wedded life not enveloped in dirty rumors. The biopic needs some good publicity after being continually stalled by people baying for Vikram's blood. All of these reasons, I believe, should appeal to your good sense."

"What if I still harbor hatred for you over how you threw me over a decade ago when greener pastures called? What if I take this chance to tumble you into love, and ruin you once and for all? What if—"

"I didn't throw you over for any…" she faltered, the resolute conviction in his gaze stealing away her words. For a few seconds, Zara had no idea what to even say. What was he talking about? She wanted to demand he explain what he meant by that. But he wouldn't. She knew that from the wicked look in his eyes. It was abundantly clear that he would enjoy seeing her squirm if she asked him. "It seems we see the past differently," she said carefully, unable to curb those words. She didn't give him a chance to say more. "Do I wonder why you're constantly getting involved with unsuitable women? Yes. But do I worry that you've become a man who would find pleasure in a woman's pain, in my pain? Never.

"As we get older, we become better prepared to deal with the world, we start wearing masks, we hide our fears, but at the core, we remain who we've always been. Isn't that the gist of your national award–winning movie?"

"A woman with all the answers," Virat said, finding comfort in her innate trust in him, despite everything. Maybe the fact that the entire world—including his mother—thought him a dangerous seducer of innocents had begun to grate. He was a rebel at heart but not how the world imagined it.

He was a decade older, wiser, and more cynical. The whole world thought him brilliant. And he was the first to admit he had a unique point of view. But that knowledge had come at a high price.

The more he saw of the world, the less he wanted to be vulnerable in front of it. It was only through the medium of film that he could share parts of himself. Truly, it was a lesson he'd been taught even as a nine-year-old boy, when his father had shown up for both Vikram and their younger sister, Anya, at the annual school day, but not for Virat. And at sixteen, when his father had called him his mother's not so little dirty secret.

When he'd met Zara, he'd thought he'd met a kindred soul. A woman who was also looking for a place to belong. But Zara had proved to him that he wasn't enough for what she wanted, only confirming what he'd always known about himself. He wasn't good enough to be a Raawal.

And yet when Virat had stopped trying to please others, he'd found his own power. In his art and in his career. And in his personal life.

"No one really appreciates what it takes to be a well-informed woman," she said with a long-suffering sigh.

He smiled. He shouldn't be surprised that it was easy to talk to her. They had always had an inexplicable connection. An undeniable chemistry. A strange sort of magic happened whenever they came together.

After her screen test for the biopic—Virat wasn't going to hire anyone without one—Bhai had seen the kind of performance Zara was capable of giving in Virat's hands. He'd had to needle her, push her, draw her out to give her best to the role. Consummate professional that she was, she'd taken every criticism and suggestion he'd made with a grace he'd rarely seen on a film set.

And in the end, when Zara had tried that scene again, she'd been vibrating with energy and nuance. She'd been magnificent. Ever the businessman, his brother was counting on that alchemy to show up on the screen. With Virat at the helm and Bhai and Zara on screen, Virat had no doubt the movie would be extraordinary.

His own magnum opus. His legacy.

He couldn't give up on the docuseries he'd started secretly filming that would expose the dirty underbelly of a lot of powerful men, but he didn't want to miss the chance to add his name to the Raawal legacy.

Zara had hit the nail on its head. That she'd so clearly known what would motivate him to behave was like a thorn stuck under his skin. He didn't want to be aware of how perceptive she could be when it came to him. He didn't want her in his life at all. But since he was responsible for the rumors surrounding him and the minister's wife, who was actually helping him to bring down her abusive husband, not sleeping with Virat like everyone believed, and because he did care about his brother and Naina, he would behave.

Because this served him, as well. And because, as he was discovering, there was a lot of fun to be had in tripping Zara's confidence. In poking at the Queen's untouchable poise. Already there was that slight buzz in his blood from just parrying words with her.

"If you're signing up to be my keeper," he said, meeting her eyes again, "the woman who will transform me from being a marriage-wrecking womanizer to someone totally respectable, you should know I'm not as malleable as I used to be."

Color seeped into her cheeks but she held his gaze boldly. "You, malleable? Virat, you are the most intense man I have ever met. Even at twenty, there was this...energy about you. This vitality. This thirst to prove yourself to the world.

"Maybe your memories are skewed. Maybe

you've even convinced yourself that I took advantage of a younger man. But I remember otherwise."

"Do you? Remember, that is?" Curiosity overcame his resentment.

"I do. Regularly," she said vehemently and then blushed. Her lashes fluttered down, her silky hair cooperatively falling onto her face. Her honesty added to that hum under his skin.

He held her gaze. "A fake romance where I end up dumping you in a few weeks' time is only going to make me even more the villain. It's bad enough your entire fandom thinks Bhai traded you in for a younger model. I can just imagine the headlines if they thought I was playing with you, too—'Raawal Brothers bounce Zara Khan between them' or some such rot." He let his words sink in. "If this is to have the immediate positive impact we want it to have, we should announce our engagement."

"Absolutely not!" Her stubborn mouth drew into a line, her eyes flashing fire. "An engagement is a step too far, Virat. I… Maybe you have no plans for your future other than playing games with other men's wives, but I…"

"You what, Zara? You're still waiting for your prince? Still waiting for your happily-ever-after?"

She flinched and looked away, and Virat felt a moment's tenderness for her. Which was entirely misguided. He was still bitter about what she'd done ten years ago, but now he'd had years of experience working in the film industry, he did at least understand how valuable networking was if you wanted to get anywhere.

But nevertheless, he wasn't ever going to buy into those flashes of vulnerability he glimpsed in her eyes sometimes. Not again.

"Think of it, Zara. If you truly want to pull the negative attention away from Bhai and Naina's wedding next week, if you want to create some good PR for the biopic, then logically our engagement provides you with better value. Like Bhai's super-sentimental sagas where you get action, drama and the romance of a lifetime all wrapped up in one," he said, mimicking the reviews of Vikram's last blockbuster.

A smile peeked from the edges of her mouth and she sighed. "Fine. You always could get me with your logic."

He shrugged. "It makes sense. The minister and his powerful cronies will be distracted by my beautiful fiancée, who's taming me away from their young wives. Once the biopic releases, we can slowly untangle from each other, pretending we both made a mistake."

"I'm sure they're all going to pray that I have the power to make you stay with me. Really, Virat, of all the things I expected from you, this wasn't—"

He leaned forward on the table and Zara felt the force of his attention like a laser beam. "And what is that, *shahzadi*? What were your expectations of me? I've been waiting for a long time to hear them."

The intensity of his softly spoken words played

on Zara's skin. Maybe he wasn't a completely different man. Maybe he'd just learned to mask all that emotional turmoil better. "Playing games with powerful men's innocent twenty-year-old wives… that was the last thing I expected of you."

Fury flared in his eyes but he banked it with an ease he hadn't possessed before. "Of all the shortcomings I attributed to you, *shahzadi*, hypocrisy wasn't one of them."

"I'm not moralizing to you, Virat. I'm just—"

"You and I both know innocence is not a measure of age, Zara. You had no problem having wild sex with me when I was barely twenty."

"That's different. I'm only five years older than you and you were never simply an innocent, and…" Zara said, flushing at the blunt way he put it. "I… you…we meant something to each other."

"Did we?" Again, two soft words but with a wealth of emotion brimming beneath them. "Have you revised our entire history together into some romantic fairy tale, Zara?"

His question contained a strange mixture of contempt and pity. Again, Zara had the feeling she was walking through a minefield. Blindfolded. "It did mean something to me. It meant a great deal," she replied, refusing to look away. As if she'd done something wrong. "And I'm not going to sit here and let you twist and manipulate our past into something lurid and dirty. This will never work if you make me out to be some vampy villainess that…"

Whatever his earlier comments, he surprised her

into silence by taking her hand in his, the pads of his thumbs more abrasive than the rough grain of the solid oak of the table, from years of playing stringed instruments. The man could strum women with the same ease. "You're right. The past is done with."

Zara fought the urge to pull away, and raised her brows in question.

The very devil danced in his eyes, sending a shiver down her spine.

"So we're agreed, then?" he asked now, all politeness and easy smile. "We'll announce our engagement, maybe tomorrow at the awards show. And then arrive at Bhai's wedding together next week."

Zara nodded, a strange cocktail of apprehension and excitement swirling through her belly.

"Should we practice, then, *shahzadi*?"

"Practice what?" she whispered.

"A little intimacy. If you'd like, I can script it for us."

"And how would that go?" Zara whispered, some devil in her goading her on. For the life of her, she didn't want to back down now. And she had a feeling that was what the rogue wanted.

In one smooth movement, he was standing before her. His sharp features in shadow, only that plump curve of his lower lip illuminated, his intensity tugged at Zara. Then he bent from his great height and his fingers were mere whispers away from her mouth. "A little touching. Followed by some light petting. And then maybe, if we both can stand it, one kiss?"

CHAPTER THREE

ZARA DIDN'T JUMP about like a scalded cat through sheer willpower. So the devil meant to torture her for the next few months. For what reason, she had no idea. She traced the veins on the back of his hand lightly. "You change moods like Mumbai's monsoon, Virat. One second, you're ripping into me and the next, touching me as if you can't stop."

"There's a man with his cell phone camera trained on us behind the bar." His voice was a husky whisper over the rim of her ear. "Look at me as if you can't get enough of me, *shahzadi*."

Zara's belly swooped on a wave of disappointment. But if he thought she was going to act like the scared mouse she'd been ten years ago, he was in for a shock. And if her memory served her right, Virat had been such a cynical soul even back then that he'd adored anything that could shock him.

Zara leaned forward on her barstool, pressed her hand to his chest and looked up. With his jacket discarded, the fabric of his shirt was no barrier to the thud of his heart or the warmth of his body under her palm. "Should this give him the perfect clip of us, do you think?" she whispered, all wide eyes and angelic compliance.

The dark laughter in his light brown eyes made her want to shout in delight. Long fingers grazed her bare shoulder, and then he was leaning down. "I should apologize for any doubts I had about you seeing this through, Zara. In this moment, I might be forgiven for thinking you truly want me."

There was no way Zara could miss the bite of scorn in those words. Especially since he was right. She did want him. And that want, that vulnerability made her angry. Not ashamed. She'd never again be ashamed of her desires or her dreams again—Virat himself had taught her that. But she was angry that it took no more than an hour in his company for the floodgates of her desire to open up. For him especially. All this frantic need under her skin was to please him. To see true desire for her reflected in his eyes.

Something rose up inside her at the calm humor in his gaze, some wickedly desperate need to knock him off balance. To make him acknowledge that her presence in his life was not some willingly tolerated headache.

"So am I allowed to take complete advantage of this moment, Virat? Am I allowed to show them why my heart's not broken over Vikram's impending wedding?" she threw back.

"Do your worst, *shahzadi*," he retorted, all laughter gone. His fingers tightened over her skin just a fraction. “Or is it your best that I should demand?”

That was all the nudge Zara needed. She pushed off from the stool and landed in front of him. With the high table digging into her back, she was neatly wedged right up against him. And in front of her was the challenge simmering away in his eyes.

It was all there—the laughing dare in his raised brows as he surveyed her from his slight height advantage, the stubborn tilt of his mouth, the casual, laid-back attitude in his tall frame. That she could not move him. That she could have no effect on him. Not anymore. That this agreement between them couldn’t be anything but a mutually beneficial drama being played out just to distract an avid audience.

That there wasn’t even a hint of anything real between them. Not anymore.

It was an eminently sensible attitude Zara should be embracing, too, and yet something in her rebelled against it.

In four-inch heels, she found her mouth was perfectly placed just below his. Holding his eyes, she clasped his jaw, tilted her head and pressed her mouth to his. This close, she could see the shadows cast by the sweep of his lashes, the sharp highs and hollows of his cheekbones, the small scar at the edge of his mouth.

He tasted of rum and cigars and something so inherently male and irresistible that her knees wobbled beneath her. With a soft groan that she couldn’t let out or swallow, Zara increased the pressure of her mouth, needing more contact, more friction, more everything.

She'd forgotten how soft his lips were. How his ever-present stubble created a delicious contrast against the sensitive skin of her jaw. How solidly built he was. How good he tasted. How much she'd adored having him to herself like this.

The gorgeous rebel Virat Raawal that every girl in the country was gaga over. The man who refused to follow in his legendary brother and father's footsteps and take up acting but chose to remain a mystery behind the camera instead.

A sudden furor swelled in her breast, an urgency taking root in her veins as Zara thought of all the ways she had had him and then lost him. This chaste press of her lips she allowed herself wasn't enough. It brought back all the longing she'd suppressed for this man. All the pain of walking away from him. All the ache of a decade as she'd watched him rise up through the industry and chase woman after woman while he didn't even acknowledge her existence. While he looked through her, past her at award ceremonies and charity events, as if he hadn't known her more intimately than any other man in the world.

God, she had wanted this kiss for ten years, she'd wanted it from the moment she had walked away from him, and she was so tired of waiting. Tired of being careful with her feelings. Tired of locking herself up in a cage she had built for herself. She kissed him more urgently then, as if she had to get all of this need and longing out of her. And into him.

But not even his breathing changed.

His nostrils flared but he stood there like a motionless giant, his hands dangling at his sides. Unmoved and mocking. As if she was nothing but one more woman in his impressive lineup. As if she couldn't make a dent in that damned self-possession of his. And Zara had enough.

Her hands crawled over his shoulders to the nape of his neck and demanded he bend. When he didn't, she pressed her face to his throat and let her tongue play with his pulse hammering away there.

She dragged her teeth softly against the hollow of his throat. Trailing soft kisses up and down the line of his jaw, she breathed him in. She licked the small scar on the side of his lip. Scraping her nails into his scalp, she pulled him closer until her breasts touched his chest. And then when Zara went for his mouth again, she knew she'd finally smashed through that steely control of his. He wasn't happy to be a silent spectator anymore. A faint energy vibrated underneath his stillness now, giving her a jolt of her own power.

His fingers sank into her hair, his other hand sweeping around her waist to pull her closer. Zara thrilled at the intimate contact with his hard body. Every muscle in her was singing, every nerve vibrating with need.

"I know what you should call me instead of princess," she murmured, holding his gaze, knowing she was setting the tone for the rest of their arrangement, however long it played out. Knowing that while it was okay to want Virat again like this, with an all-consuming need, she could never let him see how much it scared her, how much power he could still have over her given half the chance. She could never let him realize how much she still cared about his opinion. About him.

She'd worked hard and made enough sacrifices to be where she was today. If there was one thing she'd learned from surviving this industry for a decade, it was that she had to own her success, her choices. She couldn't show vulnerability, regrets, doubts to anyone.

Not to this man, of all people, who knew exactly where and how she had gotten started.

"What?" he said, after a slow blink. A soft word. Desire was a glimmering truth in his eyes and she realized he'd needed a moment to understand what she'd said.

She smiled. She didn't care why she was kissing him now. Or why he was kissing her back. She just wanted. More of him and more of his kisses. "Queen. After all, I built my own kingdom."

His laughter reverberated through her own body, leaving echoes. "Now that I won't disagree with, Zara." He pushed at a strand of her hair, his thumb drawing a barely there line on her jaw. Her skin, her entire being shimmered with anticipation and want. Because through all this, Zara knew he hadn't fully unleashed his own desire. He'd let her get to him, yes, but not tipped over. Not yet. "So should I test if I can make the Queen quake and tremble in my arms? Should I see if there's anything left of that sweet woman I knew a long time ago?"

"That woman was so afraid, Virat. Of everyone and her own dreams. This is me now—full of thorns and ice. A woman who sees a problem and wrangles the notorious playboy of Bollywood into behaving."

His smile wasn't mocking anymore. Those perceptive eyes studied her with a hunger she wanted to revel in. "And you can take everything I want to give? Because I have the most disreputable urge to mess you up, *shahzadi*."

"Do your worst, Virat," Zara said, her heart thudding so loudly that she couldn't hear anything else.

And then his mouth came for hers. He stole her breath and the ground under her feet with the soft, almost gentle press of his lips. This was no possession, as she'd expected. No rough passion that she so wanted. This kiss was charged with curiosity, exploration, almost as if he was willing himself to find something had changed. To find her changed. This kiss was nothing but pure tasting.

The rough bristle of his beard scraped sensuously against her lips and Zara gasped into his mouth. With her body pressed against his from chest to thigh, he was a fortress of heat and desire, touching small sparks in every limb and muscle.

Zara would have shouted her victory if he so much as allowed her another breath. Her heart raced deafeningly in her ears as his kiss turned from gentle exploration to pure possession at her unguarded response.

He kissed and nipped and licked her lips in a frenzy of hunger that would have turned her into a molten puddle if he wasn't holding her up. The table dug into her back but the ache of it contrasted sweetly against the hum of pleasure he evoked. His hands roved restlessly over her body, never landing in one spot, making her mindless with desire.

She pulled at his hair, and he bit her lower lip. When she moaned, he soothed her hurt with a swipe of his tongue. He tasted the warm cavern of her mouth as if he had to quench his thirst again and again.

Restless need slithered under Zara's skin, the rasp of her bra an imposition against her taut nipples. But his hands on her waist controlled her movement, never letting their lower bodies touch. She didn't know how long they kissed like that. She didn't care if it lasted an eternity or just a moment. She lost herself in his hunger. She celebrated herself in his need.

And then, slowly he called a halt to it.

He clasped her jaw in a gentle hold, their foreheads touching, and his harsh exhales coated her sensitive lips. And into the soft silence came his curse—filthy and full of an emotion Zara couldn't name. It snapped her out of the miasma of desire clouding her rationality. His anger at himself was a slap against her senses.

She stepped sideways, tottered on her heels, and he immediately shot out a hand to steady her. She raised a confused gaze to his, her body still made of pleasure currents. After ten years of drought, his touch, his kiss, his body was a haven she didn't want to give up so abruptly. "Virat?"

"Congratulations, *shahzadi.* That was a smashing engagement kiss, don't you think? If I had known you'd morph into such a wonderful actress, I'd have hired you ages ago for one of my projects."

Zara poked him in the chest, anger washing over her. "I wasn't acting. And neither were you." She also had no idea why she wasn't simply taking the out he was giving her. Laughing away the kiss. "I won't let any man shame me for my desires or my dreams. And do you know who taught me how freeing it could be to truly embrace oneself? You.

"Maybe you need a reminder, Virat. Maybe you do need saving from yourself."

She didn't wait to hear his answer. Holding her head high, Zara walked away from him, wondering what the hell she had started tonight.

Zara leaned against the giant statue of an elephant covered in shimmering mosaic tiles and watched the laughing gaggle of young women surrounding the beautiful bride and grinning groom in the center of the courtyard of the palatial hotel where Vikram and Naina's three-day wedding was underway.

The architecture of the centuries-old palace restored into a luxury hotel had been one delight after the other since she and Virat had arrived together two days ago.

As expected, the world had exploded with the news of their engagement and that kiss had gone viral in a matter of hours. Both she and Virat had been besieged by the press at the awards show—where he'd triumphantly declared that the Queen had accepted his proposal of marriage—and afterward at the post-awards party. Social media had lit up with gossip about them, just as they'd wanted.

When they returned to the biopic's shoot in a few days, they already had more than one interview lined up—to talk about themselves and the movie, to present a united front with Vikram, her and Virat in front of the world.

Of course, the one thing neither had foreseen was the effect it would have on Naina and Vikram. Zara and Virat had barely arrived at the venue when they'd both been cornered by the bridal couple, demanding to know what the hell was going on.

While she'd stood there flustered, Virat had smoothly taken over the entire conversation. His corded arm around her shoulders, the rogue had pulled her in and whispered, "What can I say, Bhai? She can't stay away from me."

Vikram had stared at them intently before Naina had pulled him away. Whatever magic she'd weaved on her bridegroom—and perceptive Naina had always known Virat and Zara had shared history—Vikram had looked slightly mollified. Still, he'd added, "Don't hurt her, Virat."

At which, her fake fiancé had thrown his head back, laughed uproariously and then muttered,

"Have you given Zara the same warning, Bhai? Maybe I'm the one that needs protecting from her."

Zara had been happy to get away from all the perceptive looks flying around. Not that the lonely, foolish part of her had minded being caught up between two men who had always meant so much to her. Not that she and Vikram had ever been together, however.

It was only when she and Virat had fallen apart that her career had taken off and she'd built a platonic friendship with Vikram.

If their mother, Vandana Raawal, had anything to say about the entire matter—and Zara was sure the older woman did—Zara wasn't going to give her half the chance to come at her again. The last thing she wanted to remember was how the older woman had confronted Zara a decade ago. How she'd used all of Zara's insecurities against her to make her leave Virat.

When you threw me away for greener pastures...

That bitter comment of Virat's still bothered her as Zara picked up the hem of her heavy, custom-designed dark green velvet *lehenga*—one of Anya Raawal's superb creations—and walked into the evening's festivities.

Tonight the expansive courtyard glittered with a thousand tiny lights dotted along white-stoned pathways. Small blue pools sparkled with colorful flowers and *diyas*—lit lanterns—floating across the water. Divans with plush velvet pillows had been scattered around while uniformed staff passed out lassi, cocktails and chai.

And in the center of it all sat Naina, dressed in an off-white *kanchivaram* silk sari with a heavy pearl necklace and matching *jhumkas*, her unruly curly hair pulled back into a bun with a jasmine *gajra* wound around it. The young bride was dressed the simplest of them all and yet there was a radiance about Naina that shone bright, as if she was the sun in the sky making every other star dim in comparison.

A bittersweet pang made Zara's chest feel tight as she caught a look between Naina and Vikram, sitting on opposite divans, surrounded by prettily dressed sisters and cousins teasing them as part of another fun ritual. There was nothing but pure adoration, nothing but the deepest form of love in that look.

Once upon a time, Virat had looked at her with that open affection and she had basked in it. Had come out of the shell she'd built around herself during her disastrous marriage.

She laughed when music broke out over cleverly hidden speakers and Vikram dragged his shy fiancée into a slow beat. Zara joined in the group surrounding them, even as her heart felt heavy in her chest. Today, of all days, it was hard to pretend that the past didn't still have its talons sunk into her, hadn't made her build a cage around her heart.

Hard to act as if she was only the successful, bold-as-brass actress and businesswoman the world knew her to be and nothing more. Hard to lie to herself that sometimes she wasn't achingly lonely. Like now, being surrounded by so much love and happiness.

Heat prickled across her skin, and she looked up. Like a magnet seeking its true north, she found him—the man who had always been able to look straight into her heart.

Virat was standing on the open terrace right in front of her. Fading sunlight gilded the strong planes of his face with a glowing outline. In the off-white Nehru-collar kurta, he looked like a king surveying his kingdom. His gaze devoured her—from the gold dupatta falling off her shoulders to the sleeveless velvet blouse with its low, square cut, to her kohl-lined eyes and her ruby-red lips.

A current arced between them, even across the distance and the beat of the music and the laughter surrounding her. The memory of their kiss awakening the hunger and heat that had flared so easily between them. It had been so real that she'd seen the staggering shock of it in his eyes.

Long into the night, after she'd returned to her flat, she'd run her fingers over her lips again and again. As if she could catch and bottle the essence of him. As if she could find the imprint of his hunger and his hardness on herself.

That kiss had been like stepping back into the past. Like finding the pieces of the soul she'd scattered behind her somewhere on the climb to stardom, in her fight to prove to herself that her marriage hadn't completely broken her.

That she'd survived the trauma intact.

Ten years ago, she'd desperately wanted everything Virat had given her, but she'd been tentative, wary, passive, still reeling from the events surrounding the end of her marriage. Now Zara knew her own needs, could demand what she wanted. For a few indulgent seconds, Zara couldn't help but lull herself into thinking he knew exactly what she was thinking. That he could see how much she'd needed that kiss. How much she needed him right now. Even after everything that had happened.

Would he give it to her if she asked?

She didn't know what he saw in her eyes, but a mocking smile curved his lips and he dipped his head in a blazing challenge. Zara looked away, her pulse hammering through her body.

A group of laughing, excited young women surrounded her, alleviating some of the tightness in her chest. She took the dark shades one of them offered and they all struck up a fun pose for the photographer.

And when one of the young women looked up at Virat and then back down at her and whispered, "How does it feel to have hooked the notoriously single playboy whose girlfriends don't last more than a month at most?" Zara faked a laugh and said, "All I know is that man can rock my world with one simple kiss."

Pretending to be hot for Virat Raawal was the easy part. Not falling into the fantasy she weaved every time he so much as looked at her…not so much.

CHAPTER FOUR

VIRAT WALKED ONTO the terrace as dusk streaked orange in the sky. He felt restless at too much partying and posing. He wanted to be back at work. And what bothered him the most was how easily he'd lost control of himself in Zara's kiss.

How much he still wanted her.

Was that such a bad thing, he asked himself with the same honesty that he did everything else. Would it be so wrong to indulge himself? And her? Judging by their kiss, they both clearly had a hell of a lot of heat still brewing between them.

She wanted him. And unlike ten years ago, this Zara clearly had no qualms asserting herself. Demanding that he give her more. Indicating what she wanted from a lover.

She thought she was saving him, he had no doubt. And at least until things calmed down after this latest scandal with the minister's wife, he decided he would let her save him. Maybe this was exactly what he needed, too.

He'd fallen into a creative fugue, too. The dark subject he was handling with the docuseries could be the reason. And yet, he couldn't lie to himself. His work was beginning to be tainted by his self-imposed isolation. By his growing disillusionment with the world. By the distance he'd created between himself and the very essence of life—attachment and love and affection.

Being angry with the world took a whole lot of energy out of a man. He laughed at the irony of it. Zara's proposal couldn't have come at a better time. If nothing else, he would have fun needling the perfect composure she wore as a mask, and maybe stealing one or two more kisses.

And this time, he knew who and what he was dealing with.

It was a little past midnight but the party was still in full swing, showing no signs of dying down. Virat found Zara in one of the private nooks scattered over the palace, on the second floor, with a perfect view of the dance floor that had been set up at the center of the open courtyard.

A lazy quiet dwelled on this floor as there were no guest suites up here.

Up above, the dark sky glittered with twinkling stars and a soft breeze carried the scent of the sweetly pungent jasmine creeper that covered one entire wall of the hotel.

Virat stood still for a moment and stared at her through the open archway. She looked like a beautiful prisoner of some jealous maharaja in this setting, hidden away from covetous eyes.

They'd already paraded themselves in front of the wedding guests. Already answered enough probing questions for today. Looked at each other as if they couldn't bear to be apart. Not that they had to manufacture the soft hum of attraction that threatened to simmer over every time they touched.

That kiss was like a constant peal in his body. Both taunting him and mocking him for how easily he could fall apart when he was near her.

He shouldn't seek her out like this. Clearly, she was desperate for a break.

Except for the haunted look she'd worn all day. That flash of vulnerability was what had tugged him here.

With the colorful array of fat pillows and hand-sewn quilts sitting atop plump divans, the wall still retaining the original, hand-painted art, and small, dimly lit electric *diyas* placed artistically in tiny, hand-carved grooves in the rust-colored walls, it was a cozy, darkened escape from the madness below. The beats from the fusion hip-hop, Bollywood music pumping through the dance floor provided a background score.

He had to admit that with every step he moved toward her, his own heart matched the bop-bop of that dance beat. He was still that damned twenty-year-old when it came to her.

Attraction was different from affection, he reassured himself. Attraction could be worked out of one's system. Attraction didn't make you vulnerable.

Leaning his arm against the entry archway, he studied her.

Zara was reclining against one pillow, her knees demurely tucked sideways, her skirt spread around her in a circle as if someone had posed her like that. She had wrapped a silky shawl around her bare shoulders. From the *lehenga-choli* in the morning to the white crop top and blue skirt she'd changed into for the dance party, her transformation was seamless.

She wasn't slender or petite. Her statuesque form, the high forehead and the wide eyes all defied conventional definitions of beauty. And yet, in the last decade, the beauty he'd seen back then had only matured and sharpened. There was no doubt that Zara had come into her own.

And this bold, fierce woman who could go toe to toe with him was even more irresistible than the quiet, timid thing she'd been back then.

"Are you hiding, Zara?" he asked, genuinely curious.

"Maybe. I don't know," she replied, not looking away from her examination of the stars.

"I noticed you haven't been off your feet for a moment since all the rituals began at dawn."

Surprise painted over her face that he'd even noticed.

He shrugged. He didn't need to articulate that he was, as always, obsessed with her.

"I take my role as the naive bride's champion very seriously. It hasn't been easy to shield her from the World War III her stepmother and your mother—" she hesitated and surveyed him quickly "—want to begin. Naina's determined to satisfy everyone around her. To keep everyone harmonious. Even though Vikram has told her more than once that this wedding is all about her. So it falls to me to be the one who stands up to them."

He walked into the nook and she stood up fluidly. "You're a good friend to Naina."

A flash of anger flared in her eyes before she chased it away. "Don't sound so surprised, Virat. Like I told you, I'm not some one-dimensional vampy villainess." She continued on before he could respond, her chest rising and falling with anger. "What is really strange is that you of all men want to box me into one category. Aren't you the brilliant genius known for his three-dimensional portrayal of women? Hmm…is she a murderer or a sweet homemaker? No, she's both!"

It was this bold way she had of calling him out on his own preconceptions that drew him to her. She was right. He did keep trying to box her in. But the alternative was that she'd continue to consume him. And that was unacceptable.

Virat leaned forward to meet her eyes. "I don't think you're a vampy villainess, whatever that means." The truth of her statement lay heavy between them in the dark silence. He hated being wrong. And yet, he had a feeling he was continually putting his foot wrong with Zara. "It's not a huge leap to think there might be awkwardness between you and Bhai's newfound love. After all, you and he have been linked..."

"There has never been a whisper of physical attraction between me and Vikram. We let the media make more of our friendship than there really was because it served our purpose." The words fell into the silence with the force of a gale.

Virat felt as if he'd been smacked in the face. Not because of the clarification she provided after all these years but at the relief that poured through him like a gushing river. He hadn't realized how much bitterness he still nursed inside that Zara had chosen Bhai over him because Vikram could give her career a boost unlike anything Virat could have done for her at that time. But had she chosen Vikram, truly?

There was a clear disconnect between his version and her version of the past. Suddenly, the entire foundation he'd been standing on for a decade seemed full of holes.

This time, her anger wasn't hidden at all. It blazed out of her eyes and the twist of her mouth. "If you think I just swapped you for Vikram when I got bored or..."

He had no idea what she saw in his face but the fight deflated out of her. She blinked, as if fighting tears, her hand slightly trembling as she pulled her hair away with both hands in an incredibly graceful movement. "Of course. That's exactly what you thought. It's how little you think of me."

Before he could blink, she was moving away. "I can't take this, not today."

He wrapped his fingers around her arm, stopping her. "Zara, wait!" She turned her face away from him and he let her. Something in him rebelled at the idea of hurting her. Of being the reason for a strong woman like her to be brought low. "I didn't mean to hound you out of here. To throw recriminations at you."

Her fury only increased. "No, for ten years, you have simply looked through me. As if I didn't exist. As if our entire history together was erased. I would have welcomed recriminations, because at least that meant you were giving me a chance to explain. But I didn't deserve even that much in your eyes, did I?"

"You were the one who left, Zara," he said gently, as if that small fact hadn't rocked his life like an earthquake. "You accepted a movie offer from Bhai and left."

"Because I was trying to build a career and you—"

"Ms. Khan, is that you?" interrupted a soft female voice from outside the arched doorway. Zara's breath fell on his cheek in a soft stroke and Virat barely held his temper in check. The last thing he wanted right now was to deal with gushing girls who thought his and Zara's romance was a sparkly fairy tale they all could take part in.

"Oh, Ms. Khan, I don't know how to thank you for inviting me. I've already met so many people," the woman continued, stepping into the dimly lit nook. And then her gaze fell on Virat and his hand around Zara's arm and their heads tilted together.

"I… Oh… Oh, I'm so sorry, Mr. Raawal. I didn't see you there or I'd have never—"

"Don't worry, Meera." Her fingers on his wrist, Zara pulled his hand away from her arm. Her gaze held Virat's with a bold challenge that made his spirit sing. As he watched, she pushed away the naked hurt on her face until there was nothing but sweet charm. "I forgot what an important man my fiancé is and was bothering him with the most inconsequential thing from a long time ago," she said, looping their arms together and turning them around to face the woman.

After she'd left him, he'd no choice but to pretend she didn't exist. He'd used her betrayal as fuel to push him to reach for ever greater heights. His anger with her had felt so justified.

But Virat wasn't sure about anything anymore. Except the fact that with each moment they spent together, he wanted this Zara with a desire that defied explanation.

Zara felt the swift rise of Virat's irritation in the very stillness that came over him. If he had the reputation of being a demanding bastard on the set, he had zero tolerance when it came to the tabloid media. It stemmed from being used as evergreen scandal material every time his mother or their family or his movies came up in the news.

The whole "Was he a Raawal or was he Vandana's illegitimate son?" debate was a piece of news that had been cycled over and over again for its shock value.

"Mr. Raawal is delighted for your interruption. Aren't you, *jaan*?" she said, pouring flirty charm into her voice, clasping his jaw with her palm.

The endearment made his jaw tight like tar packed into a road, and delight bloomed in her chest. It was like pawing a predator who was only playing nice for a limited time.

Oh, God, how had she forgotten what fun it was to tease and taunt him? He had given her a kind of leeway he didn't allow anyone else. Then or now. And she was a pathetic puppy who was still counting the crumbs he threw at her.

He rubbed his nose against hers in a tender gesture that made her pull away. "What would I do if you weren't here to tame me, *shahzadi*?"

Zara snorted—he really was the devil—and turned back to the woman watching them with avid interest. "Did you settle in all right, Meera? Have you been shown to a proper room? Vikram knows you're on my guest list. If you need anything..."

"Oh, it's been perfect, Ms. Khan. Everyone's been really nice," the woman said, her gaze shifting nervously from Virat. For a man who could charm the panties off married women, he could give off a cold frost like no one's business when he wasn't interested. "I just wanted to thank you for getting me the invite to the wedding. It's been like witnessing a fairy tale. Thank you for convincing Vikram sir that our organization is the real thing. He wouldn't have given us a chance if not for your recommendation."

"What have you roped Bhai into, love?"

It was Meera that spoke up. "My sister and I run a shelter for women fleeing abusive relationships in Mumbai. We aim to empower them by matching them with the right career training and Zara ma'am has been our staunchest supporter from the beginning. Unlike most celebrities who just write us a check, Ma'am donates her time and network to find suitable jobs for the women. One of our members is an aspiring actress, and Vikram sir gave her a chance to audition for a small part in a different project. Zara ma'am set up the whole thing," she finished, beaming at her.

Virat studied Zara with such intensity that a warm trickle of sensation filled her every limb. "You're apparently a paragon of virtue, *jaan*. A patroness of arts, a charity doyenne… A true queen, then." But there was a hint of curiosity in his tone that promised a discussion later.

"Meera's exaggerating," Zara quipped. "I simply didn't forget what it is to start from nothing. And I want to pay it forward." She turned to him and nuzzled her face into the side of his neck, anger still coursing through her. "Does it make my ambition more palatable now? Does that make me more deserving of everything I've gained, Virat? Of you?"

She noted the slight flinch of his mouth with faint satisfaction. Nothing like holding a mirror up to a supposed man of principles. "You know that's not me and—"

But in that moment, Zara discovered she was petty and she didn't want to let go of the anger at his assumptions. She also knew that her ire was nothing but a shield against the hurt he could heap on her, given half the chance. "Meera also writes for *SuperWomen*. She's doing a feature on me for the next month's issue," she added for his sake.

Settling back down again on a divan, she invited the young woman to start her interview. During the first few questions, Virat stayed quiet, walking behind and around Zara, his gaze never leaving her face.

"Can I ask you some questions about your relationship now?" said Meera, her tone tentative, as if afraid Virat might cancel her invitation and send her packing.

"What kind of questions?" Virat said instantly, pinning the poor woman with his gaze.

Meera tilted her chin up. "Our audience would love to know about the man who's swept Zara ma'am off her feet. They want to know if you deserve her."

Zara smiled at the sudden gleam of respect in Virat's eyes.

"That's something I'm still figuring out," he replied, with a slick charm that had Meera blushing.

Zara didn't miss the intention behind the statement. She sat back as he took the reins of the interview, smoothly bypassing most of Meera's probing questions about their relationship and bringing the focus back to the biopic and their working together. He gave just enough to satisfy Meera's curiosity without revealing anything he didn't want to. It was like watching a master manipulator at work and Zara was glad he was on her side.

"Do you want an official picture of us together?" he added silkily, just as the interview was wrapping up.

Before Zara could blink, Meera pulled out a professional-grade, high-end camera out of her bag, and she and Virat were discussing lighting, angles and the best pose that would show off Zara and him together. She was still trying to wrap her mind about how she had lost control of the conversation when he lifted her easily—she was by no means a small woman—and neatly placed her sideways into his lap, with one of her arms going around his neck, her other hand on his chest. Leaving her face dipping down into his, intimately close.

His arm went around her waist, his broad palm sliding into place over her belly. The other hand, he left on her knee. He smelled of aftershave and the cigar he smoked when he was stressed, and something that was so essentially him—a cocktail that she was so familiar with that her nerves went haywire.

Zara's heart started a thump-thump so loud that she was afraid the entire wedding party would hear it. Except in front of the camera, she hadn't been this close to a man for so long. Oh, she'd toyed with the idea of a casual affair once or twice but it had only remained a fantasy. It seemed the wounds she'd sustained during her marriage were too deep to let her guard down with anyone other than Virat.

She wanted to blame her body's absurdly needy reaction to his closeness on the drought she'd put herself through. Suppressing her natural desires wasn't healthy. And yet, she knew that would be a lie. Only Virat had ever managed to make her forget her wariness. Only Virat who tempted her, even now.

She didn't have to hold the pose for too long as Meera pronounced them done in no more than a few minutes. When she then asked for a selfie with Zara—the poor woman still seemed to be in awe of Virat—the blasted man dismissed her with a charming "I'd like to be alone with my Queen before the hordes find us."

If he asked nicely, Zara was sure the woman would have burned the place down. Zara knew she would. Meera left after a cheerful wave in Zara's direction and a grin that could be seen from her main office in Delhi.

A sudden silence descended in the cozy nook, weaving an intimacy around them. For the first time in years, Zara felt the thread of desire in her belly trump fear and doubts. Subsume everything except awareness of this man.

"Thank you for being nice to her," she said into the gathering quiet. Unwilling to run away.

"You know I would never deny someone starting from the ground up." His long fingers squeezed her knee. "You're doing good work, Zara."

There was no mockery or teasing in this. His compliment was genuine. Zara felt warmth filling her chest. She didn't need his validation but she liked it anyway. This was a man whose good opinion would always matter to her. She'd already made her peace with that. "Thank you," she whispered huskily. His fingers on her belly felt like a heated brand on her bare skin even though the thin cotton of her crop top provided a barrier.

"Zara, it's clear we have different impressions of—"

Zara pressed her palm over his mouth and shook her head. "I don't want to discuss the past anymore. Not today, please. It's already beaten me down."

When he spoke, his words painted her palm with a warmth she desperately needed to feel elsewhere. Everywhere. All over. She wanted to inhale the warmth of this man and have him heat up the parts of her that had frozen with fear over the years. She needed him. "I know that, *shahzadi.*"

She raised a questioning gaze to his.

He shrugged. "Let's just say I have a radar when it comes to these things. Or maybe I'm just tuned into you. You've been the perfect best friend, a charming actress and a loving fiancée all day. But there's been a haunted look in your gaze, too."

Zara wasn't surprised by his perceptiveness. The gentleness in his tone threatened to knock down all the barriers she'd pulled up around her heart. Shatter the concrete she'd built to keep out the guilt and joy and pain of this particular day. "I… A long time ago, my husband died on this day. It's difficult for me to talk about… Please don't ask me any more about it now," she added, on a wave of that same guilt and pain roping together.

But it was unnecessary. Because even back then, Virat had never probed. Never asked her for more than she was willing to give.

"Then I won't," he said with that easy acceptance she adored. She loved everything about him then, the tensile strength of his arms around her, the warm, male scent filling every empty space inside her. "We'll simply sit here for as long as you want."

"Why?" she asked, suddenly desperate for more.

"Because I want to, *shahzadi.* Because we've ended up here in this moment again. Forget the past, Zara, and forget the future. Here, right now, you're safe."

And just like that, he made Zara crave more from him. More from this moment. Not the future. Not an uncertain tomorrow. Now. Just now.

"I want more, then," she said, the whispers in her head turning into words on her lips with an easy familiarity that colored their every interaction. "Something more from you."

He didn't move or speak or blink and yet a stillness came over him.

He waited, without giving her empty reassurances. And Zara realized he knew. And that he was waiting for her to ask. That this had been inevitable from the moment she'd wrangled him into acting as her lover at the magazine launch.

"Make love to me, Virat. I desperately need something real today to anchor me here. I want to feel. Not think."

CHAPTER FIVE

VIRAT SCANNED HIS brain for all the reasons he should be saying no to this. In the few days since they'd been reacquainted with each other, Zara had proved to him that he didn't know her at all. And yet, as he inhaled the scent of her skin and felt the sweet slide of her body against his, he knew he wouldn't say no. The taste of his defeat when it came to her was wholly exciting.

Despite what the world liked to believe, he wasn't indiscriminate when it came to his sex partners. He had however always been able to separate the emotional realm from mutual chemistry. Only with Zara had those lines blurred. But he wasn't that reckless twenty-year-old anymore.

And this Zara was a wholly different woman. This Zara knew what she wanted and had no hesitation asking for it. This Zara had seen a problem and tackled it head on. This Zara was fierce when it came to protecting the ones she loved. This Zara… damn it, he had seen the flashes of this Zara before.

She'd always been there beneath the surface, waiting to break free.

This Zara was the one who could topple him all over again. And it was that very prospect that fired his blood. Conventional wisdom had never worked for him. The very idea of having this bold Zara—willing and wanton—in his arms, at his mercy, made the beast inside him roar.

He calmed the urgency in his blood, giving her his standard warning. Making it clear, as he always did. "This can be nothing more than sex. Nothing else. It can't—"

She bent her head and rubbed her lips against his stubbled jaw in a raspy whisper that tightened every muscle in his body. "I want nothing but to feel you inside me. I want…you, Virat. I don't think I've ever stopped." Those words came in a breathless rush as if she hadn't been meaning to say them. The flash of dismay in her gaze told him as much. But they were real, and knowing that, Virat lost what little control he had over this situation and of himself.

He sank his fingers into her hair and brought her mouth to his, unraveling at a level he couldn't fathom. With most women in his life, he played a part—the rebel, the scion of Bollywood royalty, the director who held someone's career in his palm, the bastard…but Zara seemed to so easily peel away all those masks he'd worn. Until she found the core of him. The kiss that followed was a war for control and yet they were both victors. It was a very different kiss from the first one in the pub. There was no polite finesse or soft exploration. It was all frenzy and fierceness, their bodies sliding against each other, limbs tangling and untangling in a wild search for more. And better.

Their lips and tongues and teeth met in a tug of want and heat. She was warm and soft in his lap, her tongue licking into his mouth as if she couldn't survive another second without his taste.

Harsh breaths fell into the silence as he let them up for air. He ran his palms up her back, his fingers tangling in the myriad colorful strings that held her blouse together. "These flimsy strings have been taunting me all day, *shahzadi.*" He gently grazed his knuckles over her breasts and she shivered and pressed herself into his touch. Her head thrown back, her eyes closed, she was the most beautiful thing he had ever seen. "One hard tug and everything unravels. Will you unravel, too, Zara? For me?"

"Yes," she whispered and pressed another hungry kiss against his lips before she moved out of his lap. The door to the nook closed with a soft thud, and the bolt clicked into place. With the light from the portico cut off, little illumination remained in the nook. Just enough from the tiny lanterns to make out the determined tilt of Zara's chin and the rise and fall of her chest.

Desire uncoiled in his veins with the energy of a lightning bolt. "Here?" he asked softly, tracing the outline of her body in the dark with his hungry gaze.

"Here. Now," she said, slowly coming away from the door. "I'm protected. Are you clean?"

"Yes," he said, pushing off the divan and covering the distance between them. "But the window can still carry sounds down."

"It's past midnight and they're all half-drunk anyway. I don't want to go back to my room and discover all the thousand reasons why this might not be a good idea."

"Doubts already, *shahzadi*?" His fingers landed on her waist and he twirled her toward him, loving the soft gasp that fell from her mouth when he wrapped his arms around her from behind. The taut swells of her buttock pressed against his groin, sending his libido into overdrive.

"Not doubts so much as worry that ghosts of the past might rear their ugly heads again."

"The dark doesn't hide the truth, Zara."

"Not wanting to face up to your weakness is not the same as hiding from the truth."

He buried his nose in the crook of her shoulder, breathing in the wild, wanton scent of her. "So I'm a weakness, then?"

She placed her palms on his arms and leaned back into his body, as if she meant to burrow under his skin. Her husky laughter—as he gently grazed his teeth against her collarbone, was like listening to his favorite old ghazal. She sent her hands into his hair and tugged. "You're not a weakness. How you make my knees go weak is the problem. You're like a rich dessert, Virat. And I can only indulge in you for so long."

He laughed and sent his own hands questing up her body. Her breath hitched on a quiet gasp when he filled his hands with her breasts. Memory was a strangely erotic thing. He remembered how sensitive she was to any caress there, how she responded to the slightest touch. And in this, nothing had changed. The moment he found the aching buds and rubbed them between his fingers, she grew taut against him with a throaty moan. His own throat grew dry as she pressed her buttocks into his groin and ground herself against him.

And then there was nothing to do but tug the strings at the back of her blouse. The fabric came loose and he drew it off, the first contact of his fingers on her silky skin making rivulets of pleasure run through him. He cupped the generous globes and tweaked the sensitive tips.

She turned her head and reached for his mouth with a hungry whimper that made him groan, too. Fingers tugging in his hair, she plundered his mouth with a savage ferocity that threatened to undo him. Her obvious need for him was as much an aphrodisiac as anything else.

"Against the wall?" he murmured against her mouth. Another light switched off somewhere and the darkness was even thicker, amplifying every hitch in her breathing. He loved the scent of her—of jasmine and warm skin—and the lushness of the dips and swells of her body.

“The entire palace will hear us,” she whispered back. He felt the wide curving of her lips rather than see her smile.

“Bent over the divan?” he asked next.

The funky hip-hop music died, and in its place began the soft beat of a slow song. Hands at her waist, Virat whirled her around in the darkness and had the reward of her delighted laughter. The tiny bells hanging from a cord at her skirt tinkled along with her laughter.

He felt her nails scraping his chest before he heard the pop of buttons flying around. And then her hands were everywhere. Slightly cool against his heated skin. She traced his pectorals, her fingers pulling at his chest hair and then down to his abdomen in a maddening journey. Every time she reached the seam of his trousers, she lingered for a few seconds longer than the last time.

He felt like a man who was being tormented with a drop of ambrosia that would never touch his tongue.

“Too impersonal,” she finally whispered, her voice carrying a conviction he couldn’t unhear. A moment’s hesitation gripped him.

“Zara, this is—”

“It’s not a quiet screw in the darkness of the night with some stranger, Virat. Not that there’s anything wrong with that. But that’s not what I want.

“I want the warmth of a man I desire in return. I want to look into your eyes when you let go inside me. I want to be reminded how good it can be between two people who want nothing but each other's pleasure. Is that asking for too much?"

"Of course it's not," he said, only then realizing that she'd neatly propelled him back toward the plush divan. At the last moment, he flipped them around and she was the one falling back.

As if guided by his specific instructions, she created a cradle between her legs and Virat let himself fall there with a gentle thud that made her laugh again. He kept his weight off her by propping himself on his elbows. With his shirt and her blouse discarded, the slide of his bare chest against her naked breasts had them both groaning in bliss.

He dipped his head down and kissed her again. Slowly this time. With languorous strokes of his tongue and sweet nips of her lips, letting the frenzy between them heat up again. Her hands roamed his chest lazily, but she never went past his belly.

Virat noted the infinitesimal hesitation every time her hands were about to reach him. There was something about it that tugged at his heart. "Everything okay, *shahzadi*?" he whispered, dropping a kiss against her temple.

"Perfect. Just perfect," she said, her gaze not shying from his.

He saw the shadow of something in there but decided not to push. This was a hookup. Nothing else. They didn't mean anything to each other whatever she said. There was the comforting familiarity of an old lover, yes. The ease of no strings. But nothing more. "I'm going to touch you here," he said, bringing his palm to her groin. The skirt was bunched up against her thighs but still intact at her waist, providing a barrier between his palm and her flesh.

She nodded. “Yes, please. Now.”

He laughed at the alacrity with which she said that.

“You’re welcome to do the same, Zara,” he added with a cheeky grin.

And he knew, even in the darkness, that she was blushing fiercely. Just as she’d done back then.

Then, slowly, softly, she traced the shape of his erection through his trousers with one finger. An almost there but gone contact that had him aching for more.

“Like this?” she whispered, watching his expression. Always watching him from afar. From nearby, too. Through a decade of him pretending that she didn’t exist, that she was beneath his notice, Virat had always been aware of her watching him with this same hunger in her eyes.

With a longing that she hadn’t always kept quite hidden. And he’d always wondered if she’d felt remorse over her decision. If she’d been sorry that she’d used their relationship to level up her burgeoning career in the industry.

“Yes,” he said through a throat full of desire.

“Show me.”

His head jerked up. “What?”

“Tell me what you’d like. Show me.” When he didn’t respond, she pulled up on her elbows and licked his lower lip. “Please.”

"I'd like more," Virat said, and he could feel her resolve in the way she nodded.

"Okay, more like this?" she said, her one finger turning into her entire palm over his shaft.

"More like your hand wrapped around me without my damn trousers on," he said on a harsh exhale. Losing any semblance of control when her breasts pressed up against his chest.

The hiss of his trouser zipper was music to his ears. And then her hand was wrapped firmly around his shaft and Virat let out a filthy curse that should've woken up even the most inebriated party guest sleeping on the lower floors.

She laughed and her fingers turned into a fist, and she pumped him hesitantly and Virat thought he might have died and gone to heaven.

He lowered himself down, letting her feel his weight. His fingers wrapped around hers on his shaft, trapped between their bodies. He pressed open-mouthed kisses into the crook of her neck and shoulders and he loved how her body molded to his and how she looked at him at that moment and something shattered between them.

They were kissing again, but there was a difference to this kiss. It seemed every kiss of theirs had a different flavor, a new taste, a totally novel experience again and again. This one was full of a strange sort of harmony, even as excitement built in his lower belly. When she gently rubbed the tip of his shaft with her thumb, Virat threw his head back and let out a guttural groan.

"I love it when you do that," Zara said instantly, her mouth pressed into the hollow of his throat, breathing in and out, as if she didn't want to miss even a bit of him.

"When I do what, *shahzadi*?"

"When you let go," she answered instantly.

"I don't curtail myself for anyone, Zara. Isn't that exactly what landed me here?"

"That might work on the rest of the world but not me."

He frowned. "What do you mean?"

"The world thinks you have no control. That you give in to every urge and impulse. Then, of course, it forgives you for most transgressions—as it does most powerful men, because you create such brilliant pieces of work."

He couldn't help it. Virat laughed at her dry delivery and kissed her with a tenderness he couldn't hide. "Ah…cynicism suits you, *shahzadi*," he said.

"Oh, thank God! What a refreshing thing it is to meet a man who doesn't expect me to always smile and pander to his mood."

He laughed some more and ran his tongue between the valley of her breasts. Her long exhale was a breeze against his cheek. "Oh, you beast, I'm almost distracted," she said with a gasp.

"Almost is not good enough," he said, and blew slightly over one puckered nipple. He rubbed his stubble against one soft globe and she jerked as if she'd received an electric shock. Zara was writhing under his touch now, barely holding on. "But the world says, 'Oh, it's his uncontrollable impulses and urges that make him brilliant, so creative.' But I know it's all a sham."

Virat stilled. "What is a sham, Zara?"

She gazed into his eyes, hers challenging, even under the cloud of desire. "You're the most controlled man in any situation. Every impulse you give in to, every urge that you satisfy, nothing is done unless you're in complete control. Nothing is simply a lark. Nothing gets past the cynical shell you've carefully built around yourself."

The silence in the wake of her words was filled with Virat's shock.

Zara fell back onto the mattress and studied him with a wariness she couldn't hide. As if she was afraid she'd crossed a line. As if she was afraid he'd call a halt to the entire thing. Her perceptiveness did make him pause but not enough to forgo this pleasure.

"You think way too much, *shahzadi*," he said lightly, and gathered her closer to him. "I know the best way to get you to stop all that unnecessary thinking."

Without waiting for her response, he sent his palm up her toned calf and knee and past the silky-smooth skin of her inner thigh. Her panties were a flimsy barrier against his probing fingers. She almost came away from the divan as he delved his fingers into her soft folds.

"Oh..." Her pink mouth fell open.

Virat watched her with a hunger that only seemed to grow. Every hitch and gasp of her breath stoked his own need higher. He played with her clit, and she dug her fingers into his bicep. He thrust a finger into her wet heat and her reaction to that—more than anything—interrupted the mindless want that had taken over most of his rational mind.

"Zara?" he said, not sure what question to ask. There was the usual wariness within him since he'd never asked personal questions of a lover before. And he definitely didn't want to start now.

But then Zara had always made him forget his own damned rules.

"More please." She opened her mouth against his chest, the tips of her teeth digging gently into his pecs. "More, Virat." She demanded it this time when he didn't respond.

Virat stuck up a rhythm with his fingers and she pushed into his touch with a soft groan. He kept her there—at that cliff and then worked her back down again, until she was sobbing with want. Dipping his head, he kissed the taut nipple of one breast and then closed his mouth around it.

Zara writhed under him, her hands in his hair holding him there. Moving his hand away from her inviting heat—despite her husky protest and breathy warning, Virat pushed down his trousers and then reached for her skirt. The voluminous thing grated at the little patience he had left. Her toned thighs trembling, Zara lifted up her hips as he gathered her skirt and pulled it away.

Their gazes met and held, each challenging the other to make this less than it was. Each searching for the other to make it more. Virat was the one to look away first and it felt as if he'd lost something in a battle he hadn't signed up for.

At last, there was no barrier between his flesh and hers. Pushing her thighs wider, Virat entered her in one smooth thrust. The sensation of her clamping him tight was so incredible that for a few seconds he didn't realize that she had stiffened under him. Her palms were on his hips, he realized through the fog of pleasure, her nails digging in.

Her head turned away from his, and he saw the sweep of her eyelashes cast shadows onto her cheekbones. She looked achingly vulnerable then, her body betraying a secret he didn't want to know. The last thing he wanted was to be the bearer of someone's secrets.

Especially hers.

"Zara?" he said then, his own voice a croaky whisper, his body humming at him to move. To see this through. But despite his best intentions, it was hard to treat this woman he'd once known so well as a stranger. He nuzzled his nose into her temple gently, gathering her to him. "We can stop if that's what you want, *shahzadi*."

She turned back then and he could see the Zara that held the world at bay had returned. "But I didn't even climax," she said, with a mock pout.

He smiled, even though a part of him was perversely displeased that the moment of vulnerability was over.

"Continue, please," she said with all the grave austerity of a queen ordering her knight to do her bidding.

"As you wish, *shahzadi*," he said against her lips, before sending his mouth on a foray down her soft cheek, to the madly fluttering pulse at her throat. He trailed kisses lower until he captured one taut nipple with his mouth and licked it until she was trembling under him.

"Slow or fast?" he asked with a smile, remembering how he'd teased her once.

"Slow and deep or hard and fast… I don't care," she said on a breathy whisper. "I just want…"

Virat tilted her pelvis and pulled out and then thrust in deep. Every muscle in his lower belly rubbed against hers. She was so snug around him he knew he wasn't going to last long. Every stroke sent him hurtling toward his own climax, the upward tilt of her hips every time he moved setting fire to his nerve endings.

"Please, Virat, now," she whispered.

He snuck his other hand in between their bodies and rubbed her expertly in exactly the right place.

She came like fireworks in the sky with a soft moan and his name on her lips. The spasms of her flesh sent tremors running up and down his legs. Pushing his free hand into her hair, Virat thrust in and out, in a series of shallow movements that lit up every muscle. That unraveled the knot in his lower belly even faster.

Then he took her fast and deep, chasing his own ecstasy with an urgency that had no finesse. The litany of his name on her lips only added to his satisfaction. His climax still roaring through his body, Virat buried his face in her neck.

The scent of sweat and sex was a powerful cocktail in the air around them, but instead of feeling the urgent need to extricate himself, all Virat felt was the opposite.

He wanted to linger in this languorous moment. Even that, however, wasn't a warning to his rational mind. Because sleeping with Zara was the easy part. Their chemistry was still a powerfully rare thing, but the intimacy it forced on them…

Slowly, without pulling out of her, he raised himself up on his elbows and studied her.

Her head to the side, her eyes closed, her breaths were shallow and fast. A bead of sweat lazily rolled down her neck and onto her chest. Virat waited and then licked it up just as it began its descent between her breasts.

She moaned, her entire body trembling under him.

He immediately went half hard inside her again.

"I thought you'd have outgrown that by now," she said, a wicked smile curving her mouth, carving that gorgeous dimple on one side that every man and woman oohed and aahed over.

When he went to pull away, she stopped him. Her gaze met his, full of a naughtiness that he barely saw flashes of anymore. "I'm not complaining."

He ran a thumb over the shadows under her eyes. Shadows that she never let anyone see. "You look tired. I should take you back to your room."

"I've been up for around twenty hours now, I think." She poked him in the chest. "And you don't have to find excuses to say you're not interested in a repeat performance. I can take it."

"Can you, Zara? Because—"

"Of course I can."

He went on as if she hadn't interrupted. "Every time I think I have you figured out, you throw another piece of the puzzle at me."

"I have no idea what you're talking about."

His knuckles tapped at her chin gently, his gaze not that of the wicked lover anymore. "Ah… *shahzadi*. I think you know exactly what I'm talking about."

And in that moment, Virat realized that in this room, in the darkness, she'd let him see a part of her that no one else ever saw. The vulnerable part of her. The part that had successfully held all other men at bay for so long.

And his brother, of course, had been the most convenient excuse to do so. He racked his mind back over the decade only to realize that except for the constant rumors surrounding her low-key relationship with his brother, she hadn't been linked to anyone else at all.

Suddenly, he had a feeling that he didn't know her at all. That there was something important she was hiding. That more than one piece of the puzzle was still missing.

A cold sweat claimed Virat, dispelling all the heat and want of the previous moment. Because, damn it, he hated puzzles. Thanks to his mother and father, his entire life had been one. The constant lies, the drama, the hold it gave people on others' lives…it was the last thing he wanted to embroil himself in.

Without meeting her gaze, Virat pulled out of her body. He heard her soft gasp but forced himself to ignore it. Ignored his own body's protest and demand for more. This was supposed to be a hookup, nothing more. Nothing less.

He didn't want to be interested in this woman. Or be curious about the organizations she supported, the shelter she'd set up, the farce she'd played out for ten years using his brother as a shield against relationships or even why she'd chosen Virat, of all men, to make love to her.

Something he was sure she hadn't asked lightly.

Zara knew the second that she'd lost Virat. Even before he'd pulled away from her physically. She felt his retreat like a cold slap against her bare flesh. Slowly, she straightened from the divan—not liking her prone position while he'd pulled on his trousers. She yanked her panties back on, feeling the weight and hardness of him like an aching echo at her sex.

Her body felt strangely awkward and beautifully limber at the same time, her muscles still reeling from the new kind of exertion. For a few seconds, she allowed herself to revel in every ache and twinge, every little imprint he'd left on her skin. She ran her hands over the bumps his stubble had left on the side of her breast, the faint pink impressions his fingers had left on one hip—and her whole body still shimmered with the pleasure of her climax.

Gathering her voluminous skirt from the floor, she glanced a look at Virat. His black trousers now hanging loose on his lean hips, he was staring out of the window into the dark sky. Zara felt the most overwhelming urge to run her lips over the smooth, muscled planes of his back. To walk over to him and wrap her hands around him, and let them run riot over his chest and hard belly to her heart's content.

She stemmed the impulse but couldn't stop the dam of thoughts encroaching. Her mind ran in a hundred directions, going back over everything she'd said and done. Mulling over what had gone wrong.

Had she been too clingy? Had she not been enough in some way? Had she…

No, stop!

It was a bad habit left over from her first marriage—this immediate impulse to look inward and find faults. Before she'd even met Virat on the set of her first movie as the heroine's best friend who, of course, died a gruesome death at the hands of the villain. A habit that she wasn't going to take up again because the only man she'd ever trusted completely was now behaving as if she hadn't met the mark of whatever he'd expected from this…evening.

With a deep breath, she consciously reordered her thoughts. She'd needed him tonight. And she'd had him. No regrets. No recriminations. If there was a part of her that was crushed because she wanted more and he clearly wasn't interested, then Zara neatly stowed it away.

She zipped her skirt back on. Her blouse, however, was a different matter. She pushed her arms through the blouse and went to him.

He turned before she said a word. As if he had sensed her presence in the very air around them.

Wordlessly, Zara presented her back to him. Her skin tingled as his fingers made short work of tying the strings together. Her breasts ached as the blouse became tighter, the fabric rasping silkily against her sensitive nipples. The memory of his tongue stroking them earlier sent a fresh tingle of sensation through her sex. But when she'd have moved away from him—she was not a pushover, she reminded herself—he stilled her with his hands on her shoulders.

He leaned his forehead against the back of her head, a pulsating energy radiating from him despite his stillness. "I've done a bad job of this."

"Of acting like a man who's so full of regrets that he clams up before the woman's even left the room? No, I'd say you're doing a very good job." Thank God she sounded angry rather than hurt. The last thing she wanted was his bloody pity.

He laughed then, and it filled the achingly lonely places inside of her. "No. I meant of these strings." His fingers slithered through the knots, as if they were chords on a guitar playing on her skin. "They're all tangled up now, *shahzadi*. Like you and me. You won't be able to take your blouse off when you get to your room."

"I will manage somehow," she said, moving away to dislodge his hands from her shoulders. She looked around the darkness to locate her sandals.

"Zara… I'm not regretting anything."

Zara stilled. The damn shoes were nowhere to be found, either. "We don't need a postmortem, Virat."

He was in front of her then, his eyes searching hers with an intensity she wanted to run away from. "I…you haven't been with anyone else since our last time together, have you?"

Zara's face flamed. Now she wished she'd politely thanked him and hightailed it out of the room. Instead, she was standing here, looking like a fool that was fixated on him. She let the cool poise she was known for fill her voice. "Wow, I thought you of all men wouldn't require a case-by-case recap of my sexual history. That you wouldn't decide a woman's worth by how many sexual partners she's had. Please don't turn out to have clay feet, Virat. My heart can only take so much."

He looked shocked for a moment. "I've never judged a woman for having the same needs as I do, never. You know that." He smiled then and it gleamed in the darkness. "You really know how to push my buttons, don't you, Zara?"

"I wish I believed that."

"Oh, believe it, *shahzadi.* You see far too much."

"I've learned that from you."

His arms casually came around her waist and Zara felt a sense of elation at the casual touch. God, she had it bad!

"Make sure to mention that at our next interview, please."

"Mention what?" he asked.

"How good I am at pushing your buttons. I'm sure my female fan base would love to hear of all the delightful ways Virat Raawal can be made to behave."

"Zara, why haven't you been with anyone else? Why use Bhai as a shield to hide the fact that you have no life?"

"I resent the implication that love and sex and marriage have to be the center of my existence just because I'm a woman."

He raised his hands and studied her, his mouth twitching. "I never said any of that."

Zara swallowed and looked away. He wasn't going to let up without her answering the question and truthfully at that. She wondered what she would truly lose if she told him this one truth. If she let him see a part of what made her Zara Khan.

But she suddenly couldn't bear it if he saw her as a victim. If he...treated her differently. If he thought she was too weak. Which meant she could reveal very little. She shrugged, and filled her voice with a breezy nonchalance that was hard to come by just then. "Success is a double-edged sword. Especially for women. After you and I parted ways I was too busy building a career. For a long time, I didn't want a man in my life.

"And then, once I had reached a certain level of success, my specifications for what I needed in a man grew, too. It was easier to battle loneliness than invite someone into my life who didn't make the grade. Than trust someone new."

"Ah…so I get extra points for—"

She pressed a hand to his mouth and glared at him. "You are familiar and convenient, yes." She scoffed when he made a hurt sound. "But I also knew that you'd make this easy and good for me and—" she shrugged when he caught her gaze with his "—you will not think you have a right to ask me unnecessary questions afterward."

With that, Zara walked away before the dratted man could see into her soul. And if he followed her to her suite and stood motionless outside it for a few minutes, while she did the same on the opposite side of the double doors with her hand pressed to her heart and her knees trembling beneath her, she told herself it was only because the sex had been that good.

That and nothing else.

CHAPTER SIX

"IF YOU CAN'T drag your sorry backside away from your new bride for a couple of hours to learn your lines for one measly scene, and if you don't stop grinning at her from across the room like some… teenage Romeo, then we might as well pack up and go home, Bhai!"

Her mouth dropping open, Zara stared at the unfolding scene between the two brothers with alarmed fascination like the rest of the production crew. She suddenly had a better understanding of what her high school headmistress had meant when she said pin-drop silence.

Having never been even offered a chance to audition for one of his acclaimed projects before this one, she'd never seen Virat in action on a set before. With her calendar in conflict, she was the last one to come onto the production.

Of course, his reputation as a strange combination of a pit bull and a brilliant wizard who drew out stellar performances from the most average actor or actress was widespread. The man's capability for

diving deep into his work was well known throughout the industry. And yet, it left Zara feeling as if she were as memorable as the cigars he sometimes smoked.

He'd forced his brother and Naina to cut their honeymoon short to just one week in the Swiss Alps.

So here they were, installed at a luxury resort two kilometers from the thousand-acre studio complex for more rehearsals before they began shooting Zara's main scenes.

Zara blinked and looked away, the harsh midday sun making her feel tired again. But not even under pain of death was she going to admit to Virat or anyone else on the team that she wasn't feeling a hundred percent. She was damned if she gave Virat an excuse to lay into her for being unprofessional or weak or something else. The man was a brutal taskmaster, surviving on little sleep and constantly on the go, and expecting the rest of the team to do the same.

The first few days on set had been eye-opening for them all. If anyone had expected Virat Raawal to give his beautiful fiancée special treatment for even a few minutes of the day, they were all grossly disappointed. If Zara didn't go to bed each night with the thought of his delicious weight pressing down on her and wake up every morning craving more of his expert, possessive kisses, she could have convinced herself that their time together at Vikram's wedding two weeks ago had been nothing but a feverish dream concocted by her horny body and hungry mind.

Not by one prolonged glance or look sent in her direction did Virat betray himself. In fact, Zara had no trouble believing that he'd shelved the entire evening as a completed task in his mind's diary. Not only had he vanished the next morning from the wedding, he'd been MIA for at least a week before he'd called the production team ahead of schedule for more rehearsals.

And she'd gone over a million scenarios about what—and particularly who—he might have been doing during the week that he'd been gone. But she wasn't going to ask, Zara reminded herself fiercely. She wasn't going to act the part of a clingy, insecure fiancée, even though that was exactly who she seemed to be channeling these days.

This morning, however, Virat had been in an even worse mood than usual. He'd already bitten the camera crew's head off for some faulty angle, yelled at the makeup artist's assistant and was now laying into the one man the entire team had assumed was untouchable by their demanding director.

His brother, Vikram.

Vikram and Zara had been running the same scene over and over, all morning, with Virat's criticism spiraling. Pleading the beginnings of a headache, which was a full-on, real thing now, she'd gulped down a glass of fresh mango juice.

The overly sweet juice had only ended up aggravating her headache.

She'd been rifling through her scene notes and chatting with Richard Iyer, the British Indian actor whose mistress she was supposed to be playing on-screen.

The man was full of flirtatious charm and a dry wit that even Zara couldn't resist. His interesting background on stage paired with his clever questions about hers meant she'd been distracted instead of paying attention to Virat's comments after her last scene.

Honestly, she'd welcomed the distraction of the Brit's attention. The last thing she wanted to focus on were the complex emotions swirling through her since that evening. Or the quick spurt of joy that had filled her when Virat had asked the team to assemble a week earlier at the luxury resort for more rehearsals.

All the time wondering where he'd disappeared to only made her admit that the evening had been a highlight in her lonely life. She wanted that excitement again. She wanted that feeling of being wanted. By him. She wanted him. As a lover. As a friend. For more than just a few hours.

The realization terrified Zara on a soul-racking level.

No, she couldn't. She couldn't even think in this direction. Couldn't continue indulging in that kind of silly daydream. Not about Virat, of all men.

Maybe she was simply exhausted.

Yes, that had to be it. She was weaving where she stood from lack of sleep in over a week. For the first time in her life, there was a restlessness inching under her skin. There was this disturbing feeling of having missed out on something more meaningful. This role, the most prestigious and meaty of her entire career, should have been consuming her. She should have been channeling the badass prostitute spy heroine juggling three men during India's independence movement, instead of moping around like a schoolgirl whose first crush had dumped her.

If nothing else, the four hours of dance practice with her kathak master at 4:00 a.m.—because of course at the last rehearsal Virat had called her performance awkward and clumsy—and then two hours getting into her elaborate makeup and costume on shoot days, in addition to six hours on the set, should have had her so tired at the end of the day that she should have passed out in sheer exhaustion the minute her head touched the pillow.

Maybe it was the fact that she was thirty-five now.

Maybe it was all the talk of marriage and love and the aching subject of loneliness she'd had with her mother two days ago.

Her mother only had a very vague idea of all that had transpired during Zara's first marriage. But she did know her daughter very well. Within moments of Zara calling her—for the third time in a week when she was usually so busy—she had quietly put a stop to all the incessant chatter Zara had been spouting and asked her if she was simply lonely.

Her soft whisper saying that it was okay to admit that. To do something about it. That one's career, however hard one had worked to build it, could not be everything. “Be strong where it matters, Zara,” she had said when Zara had fallen silent on the line.

“What does that mean, Mama?”

“You fund shelters, you help women get back on their feet, you take on the big, bad men of the industry to fight for women’s rights, but do you take risks with your own heart, Zara?” A lump in her throat, Zara had to swallow hard to not break into tears. And she wasn’t a pretty crier. “Strength doesn’t lie in caging one’s heart, darling. I’d hate for you to miss out on happiness because you’re afraid.”

As always, her wise English teacher mother had given her a lot to think about.

Was that it? Was seeing her best friend, Vikram, leaping happily into matrimony after all these years of companionship affecting her more than she’d realized? Was it her stupid biological clock that was blaring suddenly? Or was this pining in her heart for only one particular man who challenged her with his wicked smiles and perceptive questions?

The answer was there for Zara to read, but instead she was playing hide-and-seek with it. Whoever said ignorance was bliss was a genius.

Virat blew out a breath and pressed the heel of his palm to his temple, in a gesture she was fast recognizing indicated an oncoming explosion. Or was that when he was praying for patience? She could live a thousand years and this man would fascinate her endlessly.

"You said you'd prep for this during your time off," he demanded of his brother, who'd come to stand by Zara.

The Raawal brothers together on the set was in itself a monumental moment. Their frequent arguments about the direction of Raawal House were infamous throughout the industry and had led to them never doing a project together until now.

But to see Virat cut the uncrowned king of Bollywood down to size had the entire staff freezing in their spots. Every one waited on tenterhooks for the explosion from Vikram. To everyone's amazement, he pushed a hand through his hair, his grin sheepish as he grinned at his new wife standing next to Virat's chair.

"That was before you cut short my honeymoon," Vikram said softly, with what seemed to Zara to be an almost entreating voice.

Her riotous curls framing her fiercely blushing face, Naina stiffened at Virat's impatient stare and then smiled at her husband's clearly adoring expression.

"If you don't stop mooning at Naina, I'm going to have her thrown off the set. I will send her back to Mumbai," Virat growled.

Vikram glared at him. "She won't leave me. Or Zara," he added as an afterthought. After all, it was Naina's position as Zara's personal assistant that enabled her to stay on set day after day. "And she's contractually bound to Zara for two more months."

Virat's expression said he was going for the kill. Zara's mouth twitched. There were very few in the industry that could naysay Vikram Raawal and survive for long.

Except his younger brother.

Zara had always found it fascinating that for all their creative differences, both brothers were conscientious about not exploiting the power and privilege that rested in their hands.

"Naina will fly away in a moment if I tell her someone I know is interested in her latest film script. And Zara won't stand in the way of something that would launch Naina's career. Will you?" Virat said, turning that fiery gaze toward her.

Zara sat up in her seat and looked at both brothers, feeling as if there was no way she'd win here. But her answer, as the rogue had guessed, was clear. "Of course, I wouldn't stop Naina pursuing her dreams."

"Of course you're taking your fiancé's side in this," Vikram complained and Zara laughed at his disgruntled expression. "Even though he treats you no better than the rest of us on set. Even though he's been nothing but a disgruntled bastard from the moment he laid eyes on you and—"

"That's enough, Bhai," Virat roared, cutting him off. She didn't miss the flush scoring his cheekbones, however.

Instead of looking chastened, Vikram's grin widened. "And to think I doubted my lovely wife for a second," he said cryptically.

Zara looked at Virat and found his gaze unnervingly intense on her. "Well, his integrity's one of the reasons I adore him, Vikram," she said, trying to lighten the mood. "That and his ability to keep me supplied in…" Her words trailed off as Virat pinned her with his eyes.

"Keep you supplied in what, *shahzadi*?"

"Chocolates, I meant chocolates," Zara said, feeling her cheeks heat up.

Vikram howled with laughter and watched them with a curious fascination that made Zara extra aware of the tension between her and Virat.

"I have it on good authority," Virat continued, "that Zara's the one who twisted this producer's arm to get him to take a look at Naina's script."

Zara wanted to look away from the curiosity in Virat's gaze, but damn it, she was far too interested in what he was saying. A few feet away, palpable excitement had Naina rocking on her feet. "So you're going to take it on?" Zara asked him.

Virat shook his head. "I recommended a female director I know. She's young and full of fire but she'll do it justice," he said by way of placating her. "I love that it centers on the female gaze completely. It's not my place to tell that story."

"Is it one of your numerous ex-girlfriends?" Zara asked before she could curb the reply.

"No," Virat said, arching an eyebrow.

Zara remembered all the pairs of eyes watching them and swallowed. "Thanks for the recommendation."

Virat shrugged. “Naina’s script speaks for itself. You knew that.” Then he turned to his brother, who’d been watching them with avid curiosity. Zara had no doubt that Vikram didn’t completely buy their engagement. But thanks to whatever Naina had told him, he’d left the subject alone.

Plus the man was head over heels in love with his wife and it showed in how much he didn’t give a damn about anything else.

“So unless you behave,” Virat said to his brother, “I’ll have that guy set up an immediate sit-down with Naina to discuss it, and unless you were totally heartless, you wouldn’t demand your wife stay and make eyes at you when she could be advancing her own career.”

Vikram stared at his wife as though suddenly wondering if she’d choose him or her script. Naina let a slow smile curve her mouth and his own mouth curved wide in response. The unspoken communication in that quiet moment between the couple was full of such raw emotion that Zara felt like a covetous voyeur and looked away. Her belly was full of a raw longing she couldn’t misunderstand.

This is what you’re missing, a voice whispered in her ear. *This is what you’ve been hiding from all these years.*

The realization felt like a fist hitting her chest, and Zara’s gaze immediately searched for Virat. As if seeking…what? Why did it have to be this man who unlocked things she’d been happy to forgo for ten long years? What was it about him that twisted her into knots so easily?

When she turned, she found Virat's gaze on her, something flitting in and out of his eyes before she could properly understand it. But she'd no doubt that he'd witnessed the pure longing in her face, the dismay that she'd become so good at hiding her own desires from herself and the unadulterated panic of a second that she'd lost her chance at that kind of love. That she'd let her own fears, which she'd fought for so long, defeat her before she'd even tried.

"Fine," Vikram said, glaring at Virat. "I'll stick my head into that scene and see why I'm messing it up. And then I will accompany Naina to that meeting. She's not going to meet some unknown producer by herself," he added with a dangerous resolve coating his soft words.

Virat simply nodded. As if realizing he'd pushed his brother far enough. And then his attention turned to Zara.

Zara stayed glued to her chair as his gaze took her in with a thoroughly possessive heat. Tension sparked into life around them, stretching like an arc, as if one of the spot boys had set up a live wire to crackle between them.

Present meshed with past, sensations poured through into her limbs—him grinding his hips into her in a wicked rhythm that her body craved, the hard weight of his body holding down hers however he liked it, the bristle of his beard against the ultrasensitive skin of her breasts, and the thoroughly male noises he'd made when he'd climaxed inside her.

If someone had shot their lovemaking in the darkness of the nook that night and played it like a reel in front of her eyes, Zara would've been no less aroused than she was now. She wondered if every person present could read her thoughts. Could see the rising heat in her skin as his gaze held hers.

He blinked and a shutter came down over those eyes. As effortlessly as if he'd called for a curtain to drop. For the shot to end.

The tension dissipated, the not so quiet atmosphere of the set slamming back into her awareness as if someone had turned the sound system on again.

Zara blinked and looked around, wondering if she'd imagined that seconds-long instant connection between them. If the sun and whatever else was wrong with her was making her hallucinate—albeit wickedly erotic things—in the middle of the day.

His long stride ate up the distance between them in two steps and then Virat was hovering over her, forcing her to look up at him. In khaki shorts and a thin white linen shirt that hung loose on his frame and yet gave her a perfect view of the thick slab of muscles in his chest and abdomen, he looked like a tall glass of cold water that she wanted to pour all over herself.

"What shall I do with you, Ms. Khan?"

A shiver warmed her spine as Zara tried not to fidget in her chair. Something in his tone told Zara she hadn't imagined that sudden flare of intense connection. And that it hadn't been all on her side.

"What will you do with me, Virat sir?" she retorted, imbuing her tone with the syrupy obedience she'd seen some of the junior artists use when they approached him. It hadn't escaped her notice that the production manager's junior assistant—a pretty, peppy girl with wide brown eyes—had been hanging onto his every word and command like he were the God she'd been looking for.

His nostrils flared, but he didn't betray himself in any other way. "You've grown bolder," he said, a thoughtfulness in his expression.

"You mean after the other night or after all these years?" she taunted.

"Doesn't matter. I'm just pleasantly surprised by it."

Zara shrugged. "Apparently, it's the only way I can keep my errant fiancé's attention. If I need to be bold and brazen to keep my man from flitting away, then that's what I'll be doing."

A flare of heat licked into life on his face. For an infinitesimal second, his gaze took in the wide swoop of her blouse's neckline, her long legs in cotton shorts. Like a possessive lover. Like a man who couldn't wait to touch all he saw.

"How about you bring that boldness into this scene, Ms. Khan?" He didn't give Zara a second to respond. "You're freezing up every time you deliver your speech. Your accent…slips sometimes and sounds far too cultured for a *baazaari* woman who grew up on the streets. That final confrontation scene is your time to shine, Zara. Either Bhai or Richard's stealing the show. You're not pulling your weight at all. Don't forget that your character is the one yanking on the thread that unravels everything. For all she looks like she's powerlessly caught between the two men.

"I thought you said you'd rehearsed the intonation before?"

"I'm doing my best, darling," she replied with a mock pout, knowing that the entire team was still watching. His criticism was justified—she *was* slipping up. Maybe because for the first time in her life, Zara's attention was not on immersing herself in the part.

But on the man who made her feel so much. Too much, it seemed.

She and Virat as a couple were still a source of great fascination to the world. Especially since some of the trashier cable channels had taken to calling the news of their engagement a twisted love triangle featuring Vikram and Zara and Virat.

While that had only brought renewed interest in the biopic—Vikram and Naina, secure in their love, had found it hilarious. But knowing Virat had initially thought she'd swapped one for the other ten years ago made Zara feel tacky and gross.

"Are you, though?" Virat demanded, looking down at her in her chair from his great height. His brown eyes devoured her face, as if he meant to see into her heart.

And Zara realized he was…*angry.* About something to do with her.

Maybe because she hadn't simply answered his probing questions that night as he'd demanded. Maybe because the brilliant Virat Raawal couldn't figure her out. Because, she knew, as well as her heart beating in her chest right now, that he liked people to be predictable and easy to catalog. It worked two ways for him—because it helped him understand human nature and bring it onto the screen in all its myriad forms, and also because it enabled him to maintain a carefully created distance between himself and everyone else.

Satisfaction coursed through Zara, like a cool stream drenching her. He couldn't pin her down and it was getting to him. She wanted to remain a mystery to him. She wanted to torment him as much as he was doing it to her.

She let her gaze fall to his mouth as he glowered at her, and licked her own lips. Not that she had to fake being all hot and bothered with him around. "I'm just…distracted, *jaanu.*" She placed her palm on his chest and fluttered her eyelashes.

"That's clear, Zara. Your mind's not here. *You're* not here."

"That might be right. Can I tell you something utterly unprofessional?" she murmured in a voice no one else could hear.

His jaw hardened and he let out a pained breath. "What?"

"You were right that night."

"About what?"

"It had been a long time. Very long. But see, the thing is…" She drew a line from his jaw, down his Adam's apple to where his white cotton shirt was unbuttoned. "I've now realized what I've been missing. And I have decided…"

"That you want to have a repeat performance?"

"That I don't want to wait another ten years to carpe the diem or whatever."

"Is that what you're doing here, *shahzadi*? Picking your next lover on my set instead of focusing on your scene?"

Zara shrugged, loving that this giant of a man was indeed truly, horribly jealous. While his criticism of her and Vikram's performance was justified, it had been underscored by this emotion that was gripping him. But he would never admit it to her.

But she…she was done playing games. She knew what and who she wanted.

"I want you, Virat. No one else." The words fell into the silence between them as if a tractor had razed the entire set. She hadn't meant to say it. But her mother's words had been digging a hole through her head and her heart was pining away for this man who was so close, who was her fiancé as far as the world cared, and Zara was done fighting it.

His head jerked up.

"For as long as this charade continues," Zara qualified, blushing to the roots of her hair.

She tilted her chin, refusing to let the vulnerability she felt in every cell show up on her face. This was who she'd wanted to be for so long—a woman who didn't hide from her own wants and desires.

The pad of his thumb moved over her soft cheek. "There's that boldness again, tempting me."

"But?" Zara added, feeling some small part of her shatter.

Some unknown emotion flared in his eyes. And Zara felt as if she should brace herself for a blow that was coming.

Virat brought that thumb to her lips and Zara knew he was seriously tempted. Knew he wanted her with the same inexplicable hunger that she did him. Knew that he wasn't going to simply give in because she was available and willing.

"What?" she said, turning that dismay into a mocking taunt.

"I think we already burnt out the fun part of whatever this is that evening at Bhai's wedding. Now this feels like too much work. Too much like a relationship."

"The playboy is only a role. A partial truth you put out for the world to see," she said, refusing to bow out. "And if you were so shallow that having sex with me in the dark counts as too much work…then you're lying. To me and more importantly to yourself."

"Fine. I haven't stopped thinking about that night. About us. About you."

"Then why are you denying us?"

"Because I can't forget, *shahzadi*…" his voice was full of self-mockery "…that when you did have me, you traded me in for something better. Your career.

Turns out I'm just as much of a resentful bastard as the man who refuses to admit that I'm his son." His fingers squeezed her shoulder as if he was reassuring her rather than rejecting her. "That's why this is too much work, Zara. Remember all those principles you used to tease me about? I still have them. And I don't like the man I become around you."

"No," she said, her tummy rolling in on itself. "No. You don't like that I make you feel something genuine, Virat. You don't like that you can't pretend that I'm just another one of the women you specifically choose exactly because they make you feel nothing. You don't like that you can't fit me into a box and put me aside. That you can't continue ignoring me anymore as you did for ten years.

"You don't like that it's not an itch that you thought you could scratch and it would have gone away by now."

He stilled for a moment and Zara readied herself for whatever he'd throw at her. She didn't give a damn that everyone was staring at them. Or that they'd been obviously arguing, albeit very quietly, when they were supposed to be crawling all over each other.

But the thing was she'd never felt so fiercely alive. Fighting with Virat was more exciting than jumping off a cliff. Probably. Most definitely.

He stared at her for a long second but said nothing.

With a disgusted sound that Zara was sure was directed at himself, Virat threw the scene sheet he'd been holding into the air, called for a break and stormed out.

"Thank God," someone whispered.

It was as if the entire team took a collective breath in Virat's absence. However short-lived it might be.

Her hands were still trembling as Zara gathered her water bottle and her phone when someone tapped on her shoulder. For a few foolish seconds, hope leaped in Zara's chest and she thought maybe Virat had returned.

She turned to find Vikram regarding her with a thoughtful gaze. Naina was nowhere to be seen and most of the team had scurried away as soon as the big, bad lion had told them to get lost.

"Hey," he said, arms folded across his chest.

Zara took a sip of her water, just to give herself a couple more minutes before she had to face him. She put the cap back on and raised her eyebrows suggestively. "Why aren't you chasing your wife?"

"She ran after my angry bear of a brother, trying to learn more about the interest in her script. And abandoned me."

"Yeah, right," Zara said, laughing, despite herself.

Vikram tangled his arm through Zara's, steering her toward the cool marble lounge. "I thought we could catch up. I haven't talked to you in a while."

"Yeah?" Zara said, knowing that in trying to sound extra cheerful, she sounded awful.

"Should I say congratulations now and welcome you to the family?"

Zara hesitated for a fraction of a second before realizing he was fishing. "Of course you should."

"Welcome to the family, then, Zara." He said and embraced her so tightly that Zara felt tears prickle behind her eyes. She felt him press a kiss to her temple. Then he slowly put her away from him and examined her face with a thoroughness that reminded her of Virat. "Is everything okay with you two?"

"Have you talked to your brother about us?" she quipped back, knowing that the last thing she could do was to confide in Vikram. While the industry and sometimes even Virat called Vikram a sellout for making his commercial blockbusters, her best friend had always been a man of integrity. The last thing he needed to know was that his brother had thought Zara had dumped him for Vikram.

It would only make him come to her defense and fight with Virat.

"He'll have my head if he thinks I'm interfering between you two." He raised his hands, palms out.

"So don't," Zara said automatically and then regretted her words.

Vikram smiled, taking no offense. "Clearly there was something between you two all these years. Now I feel like a fool for—"

Zara cut his words off. "You don't know how much your friendship has meant to me. What Virat and I have is something altogether different."

Vikram snorted. “That’s clear to anyone that’s seen you together for more than five minutes. I thought I’d be surprised to see you with him but…”

“But what?” Zara asked, now curious.

“It’s him I’m more shocked by. He’s…different with you. I mean, he’s always been intense and passionate about everything in life but I’ve never seen him like that with a woman. Jealous of every look you give your costar on set.”

Zara tried to not let those words mean anything more than the fact that while he preferred being behind the camera, Virat was clearly just as talented at acting as the rest of his family. “Remember that first movie you and I worked on together all those years ago?”

The memory made Vikram groan. “God, yes. According to my memory, the best part of that entire thing was getting to know you.”

“Did you hire me for that because your mother recommended me for the role?”

Vikram’s gaze turned thoughtful. “No. I gave you a chance to do the screen test because she mentioned your name. After I looked at your audition tape, which was smashing. I was looking for a fresh face. You earned the role because of your talent, whoever brought you to my attention.”

She nodded, another small part of the puzzle falling into piece.

“Zara, why are you asking me about that now?” Vikram probed.

She made some nonanswer and hurried back to the hotel. Virat’s resentment that she’d left him for

Vikram might have been unfounded, but it hadn't been borne in a vacuum. And Zara loathed the very idea of him thinking the worst of her.

She showed up outside Virat's suite that night, knuckles at the ready to rap. Laughter from inside the suite—female laughter at that—sent her scurrying away from his door like a scared little mouse.

Once she'd reached her own suite, she called herself a hundred names.

What was the matter with her?

Why was she forgetting that she had no real claim on Virat, for all the drama they were putting on for the world? Why did she keep thinking that one evening of incredible pleasure with her meant he would come knocking for more? Why was she acting like a hyped-up, hormonal teenager because Vikram had said that Virat might be jealous of all the time she'd spent with Richard on set?

While the actual fact was that he hadn't even greeted her properly since arriving. If not for the crew avidly watching them every chance they got, she was sure he wouldn't have even acknowledged her existence.

This panicky, scrambled behavior was not her. This creeping through the corridors at night—even if the man was her fiancé in the eyes of the world—was not her.

Was she hoping Virat would somehow make their relationship permanent? She couldn't be so foolish as to fall for a man who hadn't even called her after their evening together, was she? A man who was already turning her upside down in a pretend relationship.

No, she couldn't. She couldn't let him have this much control over her emotions.

If he was determined to see her as nothing but a convenient lay—and that was what she had suggested when she'd begged him to make love to her—then that was how she'd have to treat him, too. She wasn't going to run after him, begging him to acknowledge her presence. To let her explain about the past.

She would be professional if it killed her. She was going to lock away all these confusing emotions in a box, bury them under the ocean and focus on her role.

Work was the only thing she could trust. Work was the only thing that would never let her down.

CHAPTER SEVEN

TWO DAYS LATER, Virat found himself strolling into the vast dance studio on the lower floor of the luxury hotel where Vikram and Zara and three more of their other stars had been staying, just as the clock in the expansive lounge of the hotel struck 6:00 a.m. The rest of the team were bunking down in the rooms provided at the thousand-acre studio, where they were shooting.

One of the dance numbers from the biopic blared out of the speakers as Zara and six background dancers practiced a long, fast number. Virat leaned against the far wall, loath to distract her attention.

In a pink tank top and black leggings, with *ghungroo* tied at her ankles, her hair in a messy bun on top of her head, Zara looked just as beautiful as she'd done last night at the team dinner, all dolled up in a yellow sundress that showed off so much of her smooth, silky skin that he'd felt permanently singed standing there with his arm around her.

They'd both performed the part of engaged lovers to perfection last night. But the tension in her body, the wary resignation when she looked at him… Virat felt like an absolute heel. Behaving like a spoiled jackass who was blowing hot and cold with the woman he desperately wanted left a foul taste in his mouth.

So here he was…with no particular plan. It had been easy to pretend she didn't exist for ten years. But now that he was getting to know Zara again, now that he found himself admiring the woman she'd become…he couldn't stay away.

While he also had a suite here at the hotel, he preferred to stay on the ground at the studio. He liked having instant access to any and all of the team members. Like last night, when he'd needed their costume designer—which was his sister—to make some last-minute changes to one of Zara's outfits. Having finished the designs almost six months ago, Anya hadn't been happy with his "unreasonable" demands, as she called them.

But since the outfit—something Zara had to dance in for this particularly fast number—had ended up being far too heavy for her to move in comfortably, Anya had relented and gone back to her drawing board. Or her sketchbook.

Staying at the studio also gave him a convenient excuse to not share his lovely fiancée's suite here at the hotel. The way he was feeling, he had no doubt he'd end up in her bed, all common sense gone. There was something about Zara that made him wary, that made him think too much. Feel too much.

The wooden floor thrummed with the energy of the fast number that it had taken his friend and the film's music director, AJ Kumar, two months to perfect.

As he watched Zara and the other dancers move across the vast ballroom in complicated twirls and impossibly difficult-looking poses, so many reflections of her in the floor-to-ceiling mirrors that covered the four walls of the studio, a jolt of satisfaction filled his veins.

Zara looked as if she'd been dancing kathak all her life. But it wasn't just the technicality of her steps or the poses she'd finally mastered. Or the grace she imbued into those steps.

No, this was Zara shutting up any critic who might have suggested Virat should have picked a younger actress to play this role. This was Zara fulfilling the promise he'd seen in her even in those first days when they'd met on a movie set, both of them desperately looking for a place to belong.

God, she'd been sweet and funny and fragile and had him utterly twisted in knots. She'd been the first and only woman to have made him look inward, that made him want to be better at everything. That made him want to change the world.

He'd been second assistant to the cinematographer—a glorified errand boy position he'd gained on his own merit. At least, that was what he'd told himself until he'd discovered years later that his mother had demanded the man take him on. Because she'd overheard Virat in an argument with his brother that the only man he'd ever even consider working for would be that cinematographer.

Leaning back against one of the mirrors, Virat groaned now. His mother had always interfered in his life in those days. Still tried to, today.

To compensate for her guilt, he had no doubt, and for her inability to stop his father from blatantly treating him differently from Vikram and Anya. Even back then, Virat had never blamed her if she'd taken a lover during one of their spectacular breakups. For seeking haven from a husband who'd resented her talent and her success while his own career had faltered and flickered out.

What he'd always been unable to forgive was her inability to walk away from a man who'd thoroughly traumatized his children.

The cinematographer, one of the few people Virat still respected in the industry to this day, had told his mother in no uncertain terms that all Virat was good for right then was to bring him cups of chai and clean his equipment.

Virat hadn't minded at all—he'd always wanted to forge his own path.

The memory of his first meeting with Zara burst into his mind like a showreel he'd resolutely packed away for ten years but still shone like yesterday in front of his eyes, now he'd finally given it the light of day.

Zara had had the role of the heroine's best friend—a young woman who appeared in two scenes with no lines.

He'd noticed her on set before, wide-eyed and quiet and stunningly beautiful. A little wary around men. She'd had a presence even then, almost stealing the show whenever she appeared with the bland heroine in their scenes together.

They'd finally met standing in line for coffee. When he'd asked how her day was going, she'd quietly told him that the director had just bitten her head off for acting too much.

"How can you act too much in a dying scene," Virat had asked between howls of laughter.

"You're Raawal sir's brother. You are Virat Raawal," she'd said then, a sudden wariness claiming her expression. Stepping back from him.

Virat had morosely murmured yes. If it was an open wound that the world perceived him as a Raawal only when it pleased it, being known purely as the brother of the successful, beloved older son and protector of the family legacy was like throwing salt into that festering wound.

His brother had already built a name for delivering commercial blockbusters with mass appeal.

"I'm the cinematographer's second assistant," he'd said, full of pride, even though so far the closest he'd gotten to some of the equipment had been to make sure it was all in order when they packed up for the night.

"You mean your brother and mother aren't already planning a multi-star film to launch your acting career?" she'd asked then, before her soft gaze had taken in his features. Then that gaze had swept up the breadth of his shoulders and his tall frame, and she'd swallowed. That one furtive glance she'd sent his way had been enough to tell him that she'd felt it, too—that spark of attraction between them. The sudden tension in the air around them. "Why all this pretense of toiling behind the camera? You look good enough to be a hero," she'd muttered quietly to herself.

But he'd heard it.

Smiling goofily, his twenty-year-old self had strutted around the set for the rest of the day after that. He'd already had three girlfriends—daughters of his family's friends or acquaintances—all girls who'd come from the same class and privilege as his family. Girls whose only concerns were clothes and cars. Girls who thought his name and the notoriety of his birth made him "romantically tormented," as one of them had called it. As if the reality of his life was a drama to be played out, so that his girlfriend could play the heroine and "save" him from his loveless existence.

But then he'd realized after meeting Zara that his disillusionment and contempt for the girls he'd dated was his own fault. He had, after all, sought out a particular type.

Leaning against the wall now and watching Zara perform the dance, Virat rubbed a hand over his face at the realization that stuck in his throat uncomfortably. In fact, both before and after Zara, he'd always sought women who didn't even scratch beneath the surface of who he was.

It was galling to realize that while he'd pretended that she didn't exist, his life had irrevocably changed course because of Zara.

He'd shrugged and said to her, "I'm only working with the cinematographer for the summer." His brother had neatly manipulated him into it when Virat had, after another fight with their father, packed up his backpack, ready to walk out. "I'm not interested in anything to do with the fake industry of cinema. And anyway, I'd rather tell a story than being told how my little role in life should play out."

"So you're a control freak, then?" she'd said, and he remembered being taken aback for a second. And then he'd realized that she was the first person who'd so clearly seen through his charming, useless-rogue facade. "A rebel among the Raawals?"

"I don't need the Raawal name to build myself into anything," he'd claimed, determined that this woman with big beautiful eyes and perceptive opinions would see the real him.

He groaned at the memory. God, he'd been so full of himself back then, walking around like a festering sore, his bitterness and anger spewing on everything and everyone around him. He'd been a rebel without a cause, a talented young man, yes, but without direction or focus.

He'd constantly criticized his brother for being a sellout when all Vikram had done was to choose to preserve his grandfather's legacy in whatever way had been possible.

Virat had gone about vowing that he would walk out of their lives one fine day, turning his back on the bloody Raawal legacy forever.

Zara had snorted when he'd told her that, a sound so full of scorn that he'd scowled at her and demanded to know what she'd meant.

"Never mind, Pretty Boy," she'd said then. If she'd thought he'd be offended by that, she had no idea.

He'd laughed, paid for both their coffees and said, so earnestly that even then he'd understood how much he wanted her good opinion, "Why did you laugh like that? I would like to know, please."

She'd nodded. And he'd stuck his scrawny chest out as if he'd won the first battle. "It's not something you can simply shed, is it? Your privilege… To think it doesn't carry weight wherever you go, to believe your face itself isn't a calling card, is not only foolish but insulting to the rest of us." He had no idea what she'd seen in his face, but she'd blinked and sighed. "I'm sorry. I don't know you. Please don't get me into trouble."

He'd jerked away, even hating the insinuation that he'd go telling on her to his superstar brother or his music director friend or any of the other big names he was on first-name terms with on set. Realizing that careers like hers, especially of women, could be made and destroyed on the whims of powerful men like his father, his brother and *even* him.

That…it *was* foolish to pretend that he didn't

have all the privilege of being a Raawal, even though the industry and the media regularly liked to debate if his dissolute father was the true source of his genetic material or not.

His grandparents, his mother and brother and his sister, even Papa for all his own insecurities when dealing with Virat, had never deprived him of any kind of material comfort. Only he kept throwing it all in their faces.

It was the first time Virat had met a woman who'd effortlessly showed him that ideals were often the cachet of the rich and powerful.

"You're right," he'd said then, determined that he would gain her respect one of these days. That surface attraction he'd felt for her ever since he'd set eyes on her had instantly solidified into something more in that moment. "That was a stupid thing to say. And I'd never do something so nasty as to get you fired."

She'd barely smiled. "It wasn't my place anyway. I'm a little rattled today, that's all."

"My idealism and principles may look like posturing to you, but they come from the right place. But you're right that I should acknowledge my privilege."

"Exactly. Better to embrace it and use it to do good. It's not like the rest of us can open our mouths and disagree with the powers that be without getting fired."

"You think you'll get fired for arguing with the

director?" he'd asked then, not at all liking the prospect.

Sudden tears had filled her eyes and she'd looked away.

"Sit with me, please," he'd said, desperate to learn more about her. Even then, he'd known there was something special about her. "We don't have to talk."

She had let him walk her to a bench in the very same garden where her character got killed. They sipped their coffees in quiet and he had found more than a measure of satisfaction that she'd let him share the moment.

"I refused to let my skirt blow up when I fall to my death here," she said finally, lifting her head and looking at the concrete slab where she'd fallen earlier for practice, "flashing my underwear to the entire world. Isn't it enough that the girl's death is nothing but gratuitous violence to create shock and sympathy, to justify the hero's violence toward the villain? Do we also have to add the indignity of my bare thighs and pink underwear to it?"

That night, Virat had asked a favor of his brother for the first time in his life. And to give him credit, Bhai had listened when Virat had said it looked incredibly gross to have the victim's bare limbs and underwear splashed about in that scene, just to cater to the audience's baser instincts.

Since it was a movie being produced by Raawal House, Vikram's word to the director had held sway.

The next morning, after the shoot, Zara had

come to see him. Hugged him just long enough for him to feel the warm imprint of her body on his, and whispered, "Thanks."

He'd told her she owed him coffee this time and she'd smiled so gloriously back at him that Virat had felt like a hero. Had felt as if for the first time in his life he could be something more, something other than a stain on the Raawal legacy.

Zara had always had the uncanny knack of bringing out the best in him. Of making him give voice to the dreams he'd denied admitting to himself. Of giving him the safe space he'd needed by listening to all the many story ideas that had been building up inside him for so long.

She had helped him see that for all that he'd mocked the film industry, his heart and soul were already deeply entrenched in it.

Now he knew he'd simply been lacking the kind of affection and acceptance Zara had shown him, all his life. She'd been the first one to see and acknowledge him as a man with potential.

"I know the entire world thinks your brother is your grandfather's true legacy. But I see it in you," she'd said once after he'd related an idea he'd had for a movie. "Storytelling is in your blood, Virat. Why run away from it?"

They had been together for three months, even after that movie had wrapped up, but they'd not seen as much of each other as Zara traveled around, attending more and more auditions.

Other than mentioning the fact that her husband

had died the previous year, she hadn't wanted to speak about her past. And while he had been thirsty for knowledge of her, he'd never pressed, because he hadn't wanted to hurt her. The fact that she'd begged him to keep their association private had grated on him.

With her meager funds running low, she'd been desperate for something other than a role that gave her more than a minute's screen time.

And he…he had fallen for her—hard and fast—his emotions centering almost unhealthily around her. Only now did Virat realize that he'd used their clandestine relationship as an anchor in his life. But even then he'd had the sense to not pour his feelings out to her. To not let her see how much she affected him.

He'd continued partying with his usual fast and loose crowd, keeping up the appearance of being the useless scion of the Raawal family. Gathering interest and investors for a low-budget slapstick comedy he'd written himself.

Until one day…he'd heard that Zara had landed a role as the heroine in Vikram's next multi-star intergenerational saga. That she'd already left the country for a shoot.

And his mother had been the messenger.

Not seven months later, she'd been linked romantically with his own brother.

The burst of applause from the dance master and his assistants pulled him out of the spiral of the past.

Virat stared, transfixed at the lovely smile on

Zara's face as the kathak master and his team gave her and the dancers an uproarious applause. And then, he asked himself the question he should have ten years ago. The question he'd even been incapable of seeing because he'd simply thought Zara was rejecting him.

In the three months they'd spent with each other, Zara hadn't, not once, asked him to help her land a role. Not once had she pried information from him about his brother—whose productions had already started raking in money at the box office—or his upcoming projects. Never even hinted for an introduction to his powerful family or their numerous contacts.

Even a small nudge from his brother would have saved her months of heartache at losing out to another star's sister or daughter or cousin.

She could have asked, knowing that Virat absolutely would have done anything for her.

She hadn't.

Then why use their relationship to move up in the world? Why make a bargain with his mother of all people, knowing what a contentious relationship he had with the woman? Had she thought he'd hate to be used for his influence? Had she...?

Thoughts crowded inside his head as Virat stayed against the wall. For so many years, he'd shut the past off. He'd made himself chase after shallow women and relationships with a limited shelf life, convinced more than anything that Zara had betrayed him.

But now, now that they were working together

again on this biopic, now that he'd kissed and held and made love to her, he wasn't sure of anything that he'd thought had happened in the past.

Did the past even matter anymore?

He wasn't that emotional, rebellious youth who didn't know what he wanted from life. He was Virat Raawal now—a man who'd built his reputation and wealth outside of the umbrella of his family's reputation and power. He'd invested every rupee he'd made into real estate and luxury hotels and multiplied it until he could fund his own projects.

He'd come far from that man-child she'd once known. And the man he was now was more than a match for her.

It was that man that Zara was interested in. That man she'd so openly admitted to wanting. And the last thing he was going to do was deny himself.

As if pulled toward him, Zara looked up at that exact moment. Sweat shimmered on her brow, her chest falling and rising with fast breaths.

Heat arced between them across the room, amid dancers laughing. She was the one to break the contact and look away. The stubbornly tense set of her shoulders betrayed her awareness of him, however.

Virat smiled, the challenge in her stance riling something awake in him. He wanted to walk up to her in the midst of all the gaggle and press his mouth to the curve where her neck met her shoulder. He wanted to gather her up against him until all that icy fire melted and she pressed into him with that wanton need that made him crazy.

A grimace crossed her face as she straightened

her legs from the complicated ground pose she had to strike at the end of the dance. The choreographer's assistant, a young man clearly besotted with Zara and possessing the sort of unending energy that made Virat feel a hundred years old, offered her a hand, and she pushed herself up. Zara thanked him with a bright smile but the young scamp didn't let go of her hand. He was complimenting her, clearly, as the color in her already pink cheeks deepened. Then he spread his arms wide and Zara pointed to herself, telling him that she was sweaty, Virat guessed, but the man shook his head and off she went into his embrace.

You're so possessive of her that you glare at any man who looks at her or smiles at her or generally moves in her direction. They're all terrified of you biting their head off just because they might have looked at Zara for too long.

His brother had looked deeply amused while he'd explained why one of the spot boys always dropped whatever he was holding anytime Virat was close by.

"Jealousy's a good color on you, Virat," he'd muttered before grinning, as if there was nothing more gleeful than seeing his younger brother make a fool of himself over his fiancée.

And Virat knew Bhai had spoken the absolute truth. While it had been easy to reject Zara's quietly spoken words in a moment of childish anger—she'd clearly been as surprised as him at her own admission—he hadn't been able to stop thinking about her. Of how much he wanted to take her up on her offer to make love to her again. How much he simply…wanted her.

And he was tired of fighting it.

He'd behaved like a grumpy bastard, throwing his accusation at her when she'd openly admitted that she'd wanted him. And he knew it hadn't been easy for her. She'd been vulnerable and he'd hurt her. Either he forgave her for the past and moved on, or he walked away now.

But the thought of never touching Zara again, of never bandying words with her again, was unthinkable.

Tormenting a woman because he was incapable of controlling his own emotions was something his father had excelled at. And Virat had spent an entire lifetime molding himself to be anyone but the man who could hold a lifetime's grudge toward his wife and an innocent little boy.

There was nothing to do but make amends to Zara.

CHAPTER EIGHT

"CAN I HAVE my fiancée back now?"

The gravelly voice at her back made Zara's spine tingle. Sensation washed over her skin, as if her every cell recognized the warmth emanating from the man behind her.

Apparently, her errant fiancé didn't even have to touch her for her body to start melting into a wanton puddle.

The choreographer's assistant froze. Even as she tried to control it, her mouth twitched at the man's horrified expression that he'd been caught mooning over their grumpy director's fiancée. Virat took another mostly non-menacing step, and the younger man let go of her so fast that she stumbled back, her legs nothing more than mush after three hours of dance practice.

His arm reaching out around her waist, Virat caught her easily. As if seeing the mother ship, her body fell neatly against his, sending all kinds of happy signals to her brain. Her heart thudded in her chest, her entire body trembling for a completely different reason now. Zara knew she should step away from the warm weight of his fingers over the bare skin of her waist.

Being near him and not having him, and pretending like she had him while he rejected her and went off to play with his numerous exes was already driving her bonkers.

But the greedy sponge that she was, she couldn't. Her shoulder leaning into his chest, his hard thigh pressed against hers. He was a thoroughly masculine presence she wanted to drown in.

God, where was this chemistry when she'd wanted it with another man? Why did she react like this to, of all people, the one complicated man she didn't understand? The one man who felt he was beyond her reach forever?

The poor assistant's face stayed in an awkward smile and then he backed away from both of them without turning. As if presenting Virat with his back might be an unnecessary risk.

Zara picked up a fresh towel and pressed it to her face. The coolness of the wet towel felt like heaven against her flushed face. But nothing could help corral the fluttering butterflies in her belly. Or the heightened anticipation that prickled across every inch of her skin.

She wasn't going to act like a clingy fiancée. She wasn't going to behave like a hormonal teenager whose teenage crush had turned out to be a total flop. She wasn't going to…

"I'm not going to disappear if you simply mutter things under that towel, *shahzadi*."

Zara mumbled, “Go away,” before she realized she was doing exactly what he’d said. She pulled the towel away and redid her lopsided bun on top of her head. Virat’s gaze swept over her in a quick survey, and when it met hers, it was warm and made something gooey erupt in her belly.

Dear God, wasn’t she a little old for gooey things to happen anywhere in her body?

His white linen shirt, unbuttoned halfway down as if just for her, gave her a peek at those tight pecs and the sparse, soft chest hair she loved running her fingers over. His light blue jeans hung low on those lean hips. His hair looked all kinds of rumpled and he looked deliciously ruffled. Just how she liked him.

“Stop terrifying everyone on set,” she said, adopting a no-nonsense tone. “I don’t want any of them to think they can’t be honest with me because of your angry shadow hovering nearby. That young man you just scared away spent hours helping me get my posture and moves straight.”

He looked behind him as if to check if the terrified man was still there. “But I haven’t hovered around you at all. In fact, despite being the man you’re happily engaged to, the man you should be…frolicking with, I never even get a chance to hover around you because there’s always some guy taking my place and doing my job already.”

Zara rolled her eyes, and bit her lip to stop smiling. “You’re a workaholic. Do you even know how to frolic?” It had been like this between them once. She’d always taken herself and life far too seriously and he would come in like a storm and make her smile.

"Ah, now you're just hurting me, Zara. As you very well know, professional frolicking was a career choice I considered seriously back in the day. But coming back to everyone on the set, I agree, it's not your fault that you're so beautiful and lovely that they all want to be near you. I didn't realize until now you're one of those people who make everyone else want to be better, do better."

"Beautiful and lovely?" Zara threw back, even as her heart was doing somersaults in her chest. On the surface, those weren't compliments she needed. But Virat had always had high standards. The fool she was, she felt as if she'd won some kind of medal because he approved of her. "All these compliments when you've barely looked at me these past weeks on set, I feel like the sacrificial goat. You're here to fire me, aren't you?"

"Then I'll have a mutiny on my hands, no? You and Bhai are doing such a good job of keeping everyone calm when I terrify them."

It always came back to Vikram and her, for him, Zara realized suddenly. Not because Virat mistrusted his brother. But because for his entire life, Virat had been measured against Vikram by their father and found wanting.

Her actions ten years ago had hurt him. Very badly. That much was becoming clear. It didn't matter whether she'd done it on purpose or not. To him, she'd been the only woman he'd let close and yet, she'd ended up being the one who'd betrayed him.

"Well, it would be nice if you didn't bark orders at the staff and glower at anyone who looked at me. You're doing a really good job of making them think you're gaga over me."

He scowled. "Has anyone been bothering you because they can't take it out on me?"

"Of course not," Zara said, reminding herself that his concern over her was not romantic. More of a basic human decency kind of thing that he'd always been good at. "I don't want to be…associated with the grumpy bear that they all call you."

"Ah, but it's too late to break off your association with me, *shahzadi*."

Zara raised a brow. "I'm not the one breaking our agreement already. But I guess I have to give you points for discretion. For not making a joke out of me."

He frowned. "I have no idea what you're talking about."

Sheer frustration made Zara throw the towel at him. Which he caught deftly and threw into the neat little basket nearby. The thud-thud of her heart made Zara realize that the dance studio was suddenly empty.

Everyone had quietly filed out at one look from him. The man had too much power on set, but she refused to be one of the people who were so overwhelmed by his talent that they let him walk all over them. Overwhelmed by the sheer force of the masculinity he was focusing on her right now, though…yes.

"What do you want, Virat?" She checked her watch and frowned. "In fact, how are you still awake? It's barely six a.m. and you're a nocturnal creature that doesn't rise until noon on off-shoot days."

"I didn't go to bed at all."

Zara looked away, a swooping feeling in her belly. First he'd ignored her. Then he had some woman in his room. And yet, she had no right to complain. No right to demand anything from him.

But she wanted more.

The niggling demand was only a whisper in her heart right now. Soon, it was going to turn into a roar and she had no idea how to arrest it. Or how to pretend for another decade that Virat Raawal would always be the man who brought her to life with just one look.

But of course, the blasted man surprised her in this, too. "Ask me, Zara."

"Ask you what, Virat?" she said on a soft whisper that took everything she had to form.

"Anything. Whatever you want."

The past hovered between them, like a specter they would never be rid of.

You traded me in…

His words from earlier poked at her. Taunted her. And yet, the last thing Zara wanted right now was to fracture this truce he was offering. Clearly, he'd decided to leave the past where it belonged.

Should she make an effort to leave it, too, when this fake engagement was nothing but temporary?

Should she leave behind the niggling discomfort that if they didn't address the past, Virat would always look at her as if she'd betrayed him? She should look him in the eye and explain why she'd done what she'd done. He'd understand, wouldn't he?

But Zara didn't have the energy to fight with him right now. More important, she didn't want to lose the chance to be with him, for however brief a time. Maybe she'd always be a coward, then.

Tugged as if by some rope, Zara found herself caught in his gaze. This close, she could see two days' worth of beard on his cheek. The tiredness in his gaze. The deep grooves around his mouth.

"You look exhausted," she said, reaching out with a finger toward the line of his jaw.

"So do you, Zara. I've been a beast to you, haven't I?"

"You mean, you've treated me like you'd treat any other actress, demanding impossible standards of achievement so that I can pull off the performance of a lifetime in your film? Yes."

He laughed.

She pulled away as soon as the pad of her finger touched his skin. But he caught her wrist and pressed his face into her palm and something burst open wide in her chest. Some feeling she couldn't cage anymore.

Take the risk, Zara. Ask for what you demand from life. From him, a voice whispered in her head, and Zara took the plunge.

"I came by the other night to talk to you. There was a woman laughing inside your suite. Vikram told me he saw you sneak the minister's wife out early the next morning."

His expression didn't change at all. He looked just as unfazed. "Ah...so that's why Naina's been working so hard to keep Bhai away from me. He wants to have a go at me because he's worried I'm a cheating bastard who doesn't deserve you."

"Everything's a game to you, isn't it?"

"And here I thought you were the only woman who understood my tormented soul, *shahzadi*."

He looked down and Zara knew he saw the wet sheen in her eyes. But she didn't give a damn anymore. Pretending like she wasn't affected by what he did had always been simply a sop to her ego. A pretense. But she was tired of acting as if he didn't matter to her.

Only a quiet stillness in his body betrayed his tension at her expression. He bent forward and his nose pressed into the crook of her neck and Zara felt electrified by the touch. "I'd rather see you punch my lights out than cry because of me. I'm not worth your tears, Zara."

"No man is worth my tears. I've always tried to tell myself that."

"That's my Queen, then."

Zara took in a rough breath and closed her eyes.

She opened them to find him caging her body with his broad one. Her breath was filled with the scent of him, infusing every little corner. Her fingers crawled into his hair and she tugged roughly, wanting him closer, needing to burrow into him. It was a strange thing that she'd seek comfort from him, when he could become the very thing that might truly break her.

"Why was she in your room, Virat?"

"She was scared. I've been doing a docuseries on powerful men and all the abuse they heap on women under their very protection. My supposed affair with her was nothing but a cover for our frequent meetings. She gives me information on the various women in his life he exerts that power over and I provide her with a much-needed dose of courage and motivation to leave the man."

"A docuseries? Against powerful men?" Fear was an acidic thing in her throat.

"Hmm. So far, I have a high court judge and the minister."

"And you plan to do what? Expose these men?"

He shrugged. "Something like that. She's in a fragile place right now. I told her you'll reach out to her. I know it's an imposition but if you can take her under your wing and help her understand that her life is only beginning..."

Zara tucked her fingers under his chin and tilted it up, to look into his eyes. "Not even Vikram knows what you're really up to, does he?"

"Bhai has enough on his plate without me becoming another liability. This project will be under my own banner. Not Raawal House's."

"Because you think he wouldn't approve?"

He smiled then, a soft light awakening in his eyes. "Because it's a risk. In many ways. Bhai has earned the freedom to not have to deal with any more problems created by the rest of us."

"But you trust me enough to look after this girl?" Zara asked, hope fluttering like a persistently stubborn thing in her chest.

"Why wouldn't I? You're clearly experienced and interested in helping out these women."

Zara nodded and looked away, afraid that if she even let one tear out, there'd be no stopping the rest. She'd no idea why she was feeling this emotional. But she was.

With his perceptive gaze, Virat noted her state. But thankfully, he said nothing about it. "Shall we get to the most relevant thing in all of this? I know the world thinks I'm totally uncaring but I do have standards, *shahzadi*."

"You and she have never…then?"

Distaste etched around his mouth. "She's caught in an unhappy, powerless marriage with an abusive husband. The last thing I'd do is take advantage of her."

"And she showed up here at the hotel, in your suite that night. I'm guessing to confront you about the news of our engagement."

His eyes were intent on her face. "How do you know that?"

"She's fixated on you as her way out of an unhealthy relationship. Probably even believes that she loves you."

He regarded her with an intensity that made Zara feel naked to her soul. "How do you understand her so well? If I didn't know you better, I'd have thought you'd overheard our conversation."

Zara felt as if she was teetering right on the precipice of something. But she pushed the feeling away with a shrug. "Never mind how I know. I hope you let her down easy, Virat."

"Such little faith in me, Zara?" Zara didn't know what he saw in her eyes but when he spoke again, there was no such mockery in his voice anymore. "He married her when she was nineteen. The girl has no idea what freedom feels like. I told her the last thing she needs is another control freak like me in her life. Then she said something about you."

"What?"

"She said she felt sorry for you."

Zara raised a brow. "Why?"

"Because you have to deal with me, I suppose." He nuzzled into her neck and Zara thought she might melt right there. "And I told her you had me so thoroughly wrapped up around your little finger that she should worry about me. That you're the strongest woman I've ever met. I had her barely out the door when Anya showed up after an early morning flight. We had to finalize your new costume and then I had a meeting with the set designer."

Her gaze rested on the blue shadows under his eyes, and yet, there was no dimming the vitality the man gave off by just occupying a space. "So I was wrong about you, then."

"About what?"

"I thought you'd agreed so easily to our fake engagement because it would give you the perfect chance to torment me."

"But?"

"But you did it because your alleged affair with this woman was bringing you too much attention. You didn't dare risk exposure about the docuseries. And there I was ready to fall into your lap with the perfect reason to make the minister let down his guard again."

"But not every woman would have roped me into a fake romance that easily, Zara. Only the one I've never stopped panting over."

Zara touched him then. Not touching him at this point was akin to trying not to breathe. She clasped his cheek with one hand, fisted his hair with her other and pulled him for a kiss.

Head bowed, mouth open, he let her have her way with him. He tasted of whiskey and warmth that Zara knew she was never going to get enough of. Soft, eager lips met hers in hard kisses and sweet nips. She rubbed her cheek against his bristle, dug her teeth into his lower lip. The kiss made her dizzy with want.

She pressed her lips against his, moaning into his mouth.

"Come to bed, *shahzadi*. I'd rather not faint like a Victorian virgin while you kiss me like that. Think of all the rumors on the set. *Virat Raawal faints at the feet of his fierce fiancée, unable to withstand the heat of her kiss.*"

Zara giggled and his nostrils flared. He traced an abrasive finger under her eyes. "I know I've been driving you like the beast that I am. So let's give ourselves a rest and then—"

"Wait, what?" she said, sounding breathy. "You're asking me to sleep…like actually sleep with you?"

He rubbed his eyes with the heels of his palms and pushed a hand through his hair tiredly. "I mean, I'm not going to be of much use to you until I get some sleep in me, since I have been awake for… about forty-eight hours but—" his gaze shone with a wickedly naked hunger "—I was thinking it would be nice to have you right there when I wake up and we can get right down to it. Without wasting any more time.

"Also, my suite is the only place where we won't be disturbed. There're about a thousand people who want a piece of me right now. The last thing I want to do is wake up and come looking for you, only to be surrounded by your fans again."

"You're having trouble falling asleep again, aren't you?"

He thrust his fingers through his hair. Only now did Zara see how desperately he needed to sleep. "You remember then?"

"Of course I do. You work like a demon, skate the line of burnout and then you get into a spiral of sleeplessness. A long bout of hot sex with a willing woman is your usual answer, but—"

"But I don't want to take a strange woman to my bed."

Her smile was so wide that Zara thought her muscles might break. “Breaking patterns, are we?”

“Finding comfort in old playthings.”

Zara gasped and went at him with two fists. She barely landed one on his bicep before he caught her. Firm fingers pulled her arms behind her and Zara moaned at how good the stretch felt on her muscles when he did that.

“You’re far too tight here, Zara,” Virat added, his fingers weaving magic on the tight knots in her shoulders.

“Hmm…” Zara said, with a smile. It felt as if her heart was bursting with a feverish, giddy joy.

Gathering her against him, Virat crushed her mouth with his. Zara could feel his heart thumping against her. Could feel the faint outline of his arousal teasing against her belly. The strength of his powerfully corded thighs anchoring hers as she trembled at the onslaught of pleasure. Hard and warm, he was exactly what she wanted right now. “Come to bed with me, *shahzadi*,” he whispered in her ear. “I’ll give you an apology for barking at you in front of everyone, at least three orgasms before the day is out and a little direction as to why you and Bhai are botching that scene.”

“No wonder they call you a hard taskmaster.”

“Well, I do have a lot of items on the agenda I want to do with you,” he added with a wicked grin.

Zara followed him when he tugged her, feeling as if she’d follow this man anywhere. If living in the moment meant pushing away the clamor of questions she had for him and take everything he was willing to give her right now, then she was going to do it.

She was going to take the biggest risk of her life if that meant the man she'd always wanted would be hers, even if only temporarily.

CHAPTER NINE

IF VIRAT THOUGHT the intimacy of spending two entire days with Zara would somehow descend into awkwardness, he'd have been completely wrong. If he'd thought drowning himself in her company and her body and her wit and laughter would somehow get her out of his system, then he'd have failed utterly.

But since all he'd wanted was to indulge himself very thoroughly with a woman he was finding increasingly irresistible on more than one level, he'd succeeded.

As long as Zara and he kept the past where it belonged, as long as he could quiet the resentful niggle that she'd chosen him this time around because now he was successful and powerful and independently wealthy, the easy connection they'd once shared came kicking back into life.

He suited her this time around. That was the only explanation he had for how effortlessly they'd found the camaraderie and connection that had once sparked so easily between them.

The off day he'd forced the both of them to take had been one of his better ideas. Zara had fallen asleep even before he had, and the warmth of her body next to his—the woman he hadn't stopped wanting for ten long years—had knocked him into a dreamless slumber.

And then to wake up and find those silky limbs tangled all around him…it had been even more deliciously decadent than he'd imagined. Just the memory of how hard and fast they'd gone at each other sent a shiver through his muscles. Of how equally fierce her own need had been for him would forever be etched into his brain.

He smiled at the thought now, as Zara and he lazed on a sofa in her suite. She was stretched out along its length, with her feet in his lap while she went over her lines for the final scene they were going to start shooting tomorrow.

One more week and the shoot would be wrapped up. He would begin postproduction work with his team and Zara would go back to Mumbai and start whatever other job she had lined up next.

As he sat there with his head thrown back and thinking of all that was waiting for him as soon as this small interlude was over, Virat felt a strange sense of peace that had been missing for some time now. Was it because he had been avoiding any deep connections—whether romantically or otherwise—for so long?

Or was it simply because for ten years he'd worked round the clock and he'd been in a rut?

The docuseries and the biopic were the most important projects he'd ever tackled, and yet, he couldn't lie to himself that it was seeing Zara, teasing and taunting her, having her to himself that had got his blood pumping these past few weeks.

The idea of walking away from this, from her, and going back to his old life held no appeal. And yet, there was no future for them together. Not with a woman he could never fully trust.

It was the very finiteness of this thing between them, he was sure, that made it so powerfully raw at the moment.

"You have a very serious look about you right now," Zara said softly, her face hidden behind the script pages.

Virat tensed. Zara had a way of seeing through to his innermost thoughts that he found more than a little uncomfortable. "I'm going to leave a little earlier than planned once the shoot wraps up," he blurted out, surprising even himself.

She didn't lower the pages. Her feet stilled in his hands. "Okay." After a beat of silence, she said, "I have a long stretch of vacation after we wrap this up. I've been pushing myself too much recently. If you let me know what your schedule looks like, I'll come see you. As and when you're available."

"Look at me, Zara," he demanded.

She lowered the papers with a sigh. The rust-colored sleeveless blouse she wore brought out the warm golden tones of her skin. Her hair was a silky mess since he had plunged his fingers and messed it up when she'd walked out of her shower wrapped in a white towel that he'd unwrapped as if she was his very own present.

But as lovely as she looked, there were dark shadows under those big eyes. There was also a taut, drawn look to her face. He suddenly remembered the costume designer's two assistants working all night because Zara's outfits had to be taken in again before the shoot next morning.

"There's the audio release party and a couple more events that we have to attend together anyway," she said casually.

Of course, they'd continue this charade until the release of the biopic. He always forgot how efficiently she could manage this weird melding of their professional and personal lives. How effortless and easy she made it for him to indulge in this with her, with barely any demands on him.

But then, Zara never asked you for anything even back then, a voice whispered in his ear.

"Is that what you meant just now?" he taunted her, shutting away the disquiet in his own mind. He was forever pushing her. Forever wanting to see her vulnerable with him. Forever asking her for more than he was willing to give.

As if it was a toll she had to pay again and again for her past actions.

God, he was so unforgiving.

But if he thought she'd back down or hide away behind excuses, he was wrong once again. The more he challenged his own conceptions, the lines between them and what he demanded of her—with some strange need to see her back down from this, from them—the more Zara pushed back without balking, without even blinking an eyelid.

He wanted to see how far he could push her before she backed away.

"No," she said, her gaze steady. "Yes, there are some social events we'd have to smile and laugh and coo over each other at. But I meant that I want to come see you. Outside of the drama we're enacting. Outside of the biopic's demands.

"At your flat. My bungalow. Wherever possible."

He wanted to say some cold and awful thing like, "I might have moved on by then," or "I can't give you any guarantee that I'll still want you," or some such nonsense. Instead, his heart raced and desire twisted his belly into tight knots. His fingers tightened over her calf and his other hand cupped her hip, and the ever-present current of heat between them filled his skin with a restless hum.

He traced his fingers wordlessly over her belly, tucking them under the loose band of her shorts. Raising his gaze to hers, he stilled his hand there, seeking her answer.

Color scoured her cheeks, filling the pale canvas of her skin. "Yes."

One word. But it rang between them like a clanging bell. Like some unchangeable truth. He wanted to ask how many more times or for how much longer she'd keep saying yes to him.

But in the face of the open desire in her eyes,

his rational questions lost out. His seeking fingers pushed inside her soft cotton shorts. A groan ripped from him when he found her velvet folds damp and ready for him. Hips tilting up, Zara dug her teeth into her lower lip. Neck thrown back, eyes closed, breasts falling and rising, she looked achingly beautiful.

Within moments, Virat disposed of her flimsy shorts and filled his greedy hands with the soft skin of her thighs.

"Open your eyes, Zara," he said, playing with her intimate flesh the way he knew she liked.

Dark, desire-smudged eyes held his. "What do you want, *shahzadi*?" he asked, needing to know. Always needing to know with her. Always needing to hear her desire given voice on those lips.

"You. This. Now."

"Then come closer," he whispered, bending his head and pressing a soft kiss to the skin right above her knee.

Her breath hitched. "Closer?" she whispered, pink seeping up her neck now.

"Yes," Virat said, letting her see his desire in his eyes. "I want to put my mouth on you, Zara. I want the taste of you on my lips. Can I?"

The moment suspended between them—an agony of hope and desire and something else passing like shadows on her face. He cupped her knee and pressed another soft kiss to her calf. "Only if you want it, *shahzadi*. No rules between—"

"Lovers. Only pleasure," she finished for him.

Her shoulders jutting out, she propped herself up on her elbows. A bead of sweat dripped down her temple into the valley between her breasts. "Will I be allowed to return the pleasure?" the minx demanded, swiping the tip of her tongue over her lower lip.

His erection twitched against his upper belly, demanding release. To take what she was offering so boldly. When the very idea of either of them doing this very thing had made her shy away from him once upon a time. But there was something about this intimacy between them—something that was raw and honest and incredibly fulfilling—that Virat was beginning to fear and crave at the same time. "It's not a transaction, Zara."

Scooting down on the sofa, she raised her head just enough to reach his mouth. Her lips and tongue were eager and warm and soft and tasted like honey. Her little pants when he let them breathe and her mewl of pleasure when he nipped her lower lip ignited pockets of pleasure all over his body. The kiss was a taking. Rough and fast, it sizzled right down to his bones. "Ten years have meant nothing when it is you, Virat. Do you still doubt me? Doubt this?"

Her eyes shone with a glittering resolve. "I want all the pleasure you can give me this time around. And I want to be the adventurous, bold lover I couldn't be ten years ago."

There it was. Virat wrapped his fingers around her neck and held her to him. He nuzzled into her cheek, that tenderness overflowing within him.

"Zara, you were perfect then. Why would you think—"

"I wasn't. I was afraid that someone would find out about us. I was afraid that I'd disappoint you. I was afraid that you'd realize that I was nothing but trouble..." She trailed off then added, "I was afraid of my own desires. We only got close at all because you were irresistible and kind and patient with me," she whispered, a fierceness in her voice that made his gaze jerk to hers.

What he saw swimming in her eyes made his chest tight. Made him question all his assumptions of her all over again. She brought his palm to her mouth and pressed a sweet kiss to it. Dug her teeth into the rough pad of his palm. When he rubbed that lower lip that was beginning to haunt his dreams with one finger, she licked the tip. Her tongue wrapped itself around his digit. Her eyes holding his, she sucked on it as if it was her favorite lollipop and then released it.

He lengthened against her thigh and the smile she shot him was sheer perfection tempered with a flash of naughtiness that he wanted no other man to ever see. A little rumpled, a little undone, she looked like a siren. And with an artist's eye, he saw that this was the promise he'd seen in the woman back then. She'd always been destined to be a queen. "This time, I demand everything you can give me," she announced.

"Then shall I taste you, *shahzadi*?"

"Yes," she said, letting her thighs fall open.

His erection notched into the cradle of her sex and Virat thrust his hips into that warm, inviting heat, unable to resist, and they both moaned. "God, you'll have me dry-humping you like it's our first time together, *shahzadi*," he said, looking up, and she laughed. God, she felt perfect and he was insatiable.

His breath hitched at the poignant beauty in her face. It wasn't just pleasure and beauty but some indescribable joy that lit her up from within. "I didn't know sex could ever be such a warm, funny, raw experience until that first time the both of us made such a mess."

Her laughter rang around them but he saw the shadows of pain beneath it. And Virat wanted every part of her—both the good and the bad, everything that had made her the woman she was today.

"Zara…"

"Not now, Virat," she said. "Please, not here."

She bent forward and pressed a soft kiss to his mouth. Pleading and begging, it was the sweetest kiss he'd ever tasted. Raw with longing and something he wasn't even sure he could return. "Now, what about what you promised? Because more than anything, I need you inside me. Now."

He ran his mouth in a trail from her neck to the curve of her breast and the tight knot of her nipple exposed by the thin top. He tugged at the neckline roughly and it tore with a rasp. He tongued the plump nipple and then sucked it into his mouth, and Zara thrust her hips upward into his erection, seeking him.

He treated the other breast to the same treatment, the taste of her skin making him harder, crazier for all of her. Burying his face in the valley between her breasts, he peppered kisses all over her damp skin.

Fast fingers pulled away her top when he reached her belly, and he laughed and pressed his mouth into the soft curve there. And then he moved lower and breathed in the musky scent of her, licking the wetness waiting for him in a slow, soft stroke of his tongue.

Zara came off the sofa but he anchored her there with his hand on her belly and then added his fingers. Her fingers in his hair tightened and her moans grew in urgency and her thighs clutched him harder but Virat didn't stop until she fractured against his tongue and his name was a litany on her lips.

He looked up and caught the one tear that had trailed down her cheek with his finger. *"Shahzadi?"* he whispered, afraid that he'd hurt her. But beneath that thin thread sat a much larger, uncomfortable truth. That he was never going to get enough of her.

She looked down at him and breathed in a long rasp. Nimble fingers undid his zipper and then clasped his erection. Her fingers were bolder and surer around him now as she pumped him hard and fast, just as he'd shown her he liked. "Inside me, now," she said, on a husky demand, and Virat complied.

Pushing her legs back on either side of him, he entered her in one long thrust. The backs of his thighs tingled, every muscle ached with need, greedy for relief as he took her ruthlessly.

As his climax threatened to undo him, Virat wondered if there would ever be a time when he would look at Zara and not want her.

The setting sun limned Zara's bare limbs with a golden glow as her lashes fluttered awake. Virat ran a finger over the delicate lines of her collarbone. He hadn't missed how quickly she'd fallen asleep again when they'd moved to the bed or how drawn her face looked even after two days of R and R.

He pressed a kiss to her shoulder, unable to resist. "Have you lost weight since Bhai's wedding?"

She frowned. "Why do you ask?"

He shrugged. "You looked as if you needed the break more than I did. And two days of special Virat Raawal treatment later—" she let out an outraged gasp and pressed her foot into his chest "—you still look pale, *shahzadi*."

"Maybe because these two days didn't officially count as a break for me."

His curse reverberated in the room. "Damn it, Zara. You should have told me you were still rehearsing—"

"What I want is to not be treated as if I'm fragile or breakable. I wanted to make love in all the positions we've tried. According to some research groups in Sweden, women hit their sexual peak at thirty-five. I bet you're only saying this to cover the fact that you can't keep up with my demands."

He laughed and her gaze hungrily ate him up.

He bent and ran a finger over her cheek. "You're beginning to look almost gaunt, Zara."

She scrunched her nose in that cute way of hers that made him smile. "I haven't been eating well. And yes, my nutritionist and personal trainer are both a little worried that I'm losing muscle. But, as I reminded them, I have been dancing for three hours a day for the last three weeks. That's more cardio than at any other time in my life."

"That's true," Virat said, sitting up and leaning against the headboard.

Her hair in glorious disarray, Zara held the edge of the soft duvet against her chest and looked around for her clothes. Virat gave the duvet a swift tug on his side and it slipped between her fingers.

Her bare breasts rose and fell, the plump light brown nipples puckering up. His arousal lengthened, his muscles tightening with a desperate need that didn't look like it would ever be sated.

She huffed and pulled on the T-shirt he'd thrown away in a hurry earlier. He pouted and she sighed. "I do want to get through the scene with you. The last thing I need is a fresh rumor that Zara Khan has lost whatever little acting talent she possessed because she can't get enough of her fiancé's hot body."

He folded his arms behind his head. And her greedy gaze traced his muscular arms, his hard chest and everything in between. He grinned and sighed. "Fine. Let's go back into the sitting room."

"Don't worry, Virat. I can take the shift from sexy lover to demanding director."

She sat down on an armchair opposite the bed with a blue pen and the script in hand, and looked at him. He sighed. "Fine. Your monologue sounds preachy. Like something you learned by heart to just regurgitate in front of the camera. You're not able to get a handle on her character in this scene. Especially Mayavati's final decision," he added, mentioning the name of the prostitute spy Zara was playing.

Surprise painted over her features. "How did you know I don't like the final scene?"

He shrugged, glad to know he'd hit the nail on its head. "It's my job to figure out what's blocking you. My job is to get you to connect with the character, to help you immerse yourself in it.

"What exactly is bothering you about her, Zara?"

"I struggle with how Mayavati plays such cunning games with not one or two but three different men—the budding actor who goes on to establish the biggest studio house that becomes the foundation of Bollywood later, the British general and the solider turned manservant.

"She constantly puts her life on the line for the first, plays dangerous games with the second and takes advantage of the third's quiet devotion. All three men adore her and yet…she's far too fickle with her affections. I don't…understand how any woman could be so…outrageous and cunning and…" she whispered the last word "…brave."

"I thought her interesting background would give you a better understanding of her," he prompted.

"That you would connect with her better than, say, a...twenty-year-old actress whose biggest accomplishment is that she's convinced her powerful daddy to sink a few crores into launching her career because she can act."

"I did think you'd go with a fresh face. Not that I doubt my own talent."

"Mayavati, despite being the underdog, despite being a prostitute on the lowest rungs of society, knows how to play the game. Knows how to make all the men around give her her due."

Her head jerked up, a sudden tension around her mouth. She looked down and then back up at him. "Is that how you see me? As someone who plays games?"

A few weeks ago, Virat didn't know what his answer would have been. But now there was a certainty in him. "I see you as someone who wins despite the odds. When you started your career doing Bhai's masala popcorn mass blockbusters, I didn't think you'd last long. For a while, you played nothing but a glamorous sidekick at best, a one-dimensional accessory at worst."

"Ouch," Zara said, knowing that he was absolutely right.

"Until you produced and released that series of short films for TV. You... I was stunned by the breadth of acting you showed in those."

"You watched them?"

A smile lingered around his lips. "At the first chance I could get. That was a first-class move.

You shut up most of your critics. You pivoted your career at the exact right moment. You…made us all sit up and take note of you."

"Thank you," Zara said, her heart bursting with pride and pleasure and something more. "Your praise means a lot to me."

"Because I've criticized you and Bhai more than once?"

Zara shook her head. "Because even ten years ago, you were full of raw talent. I've always respected your opinion, Virat."

He stared back at her, something in his eyes that Zara couldn't recognize. She'd complimented him, but the moment became weighted with something else.

"Tell me what you like about Mayavati," she asked to break the mounting tension.

For a second, she thought he wouldn't answer. Then he said, "She's the most complex female character I've ever handled—they are thin on the ground to begin with. Wily and cunning and stubborn. Even with all the pressures society puts on her, even with all the demands the first two men make on her, Mayavati lives only for herself. By her own rules.

"But it's her final decision that shows us how truly complex she is.

"Her choice in the end to spend the rest of her life with the manservant—the one man who truly loves her despite knowing everything she is—instead of the general who could give her riches, or the visionary Vijay Raawal who promises to launch her as an actress, tells the audience that Mayavati is, at the end of it all, desperate to be loved. To be accepted for who she is.

“And *that* is a universal emotion.”

He held her gaze, a flash of something in his own. “Maybe you’re struggling because you can’t see why she’d make such a selfless choice? Why she’d walk away from the chance of being a wealthy actress with my grandfather’s character or the call to adventure with the general?”

There it was, at the core of it all, the shadow of the resentment she’d always spied in his eyes. “You think I’m not able to connect with her because I don’t see why she values love and acceptance before everything else.” It wasn’t even a question anymore.

Without answering her, Virat leaped from the bed, as if she’d caged him for too long. His sweatpants hung low on his lean lips as he turned away from her.

And Zara knew then. Two things hit her in the face. Hard and fast. Almost crushing her under their weight. “You don’t trust me at all, do you? After everything we’ve said and done the past few weeks? After all this time? At least have the guts to say it to my face, Virat.”

He turned then and she saw the truth in his eyes. “Let’s talk about the scene, Zara.”

Zara threw away the pages in her hand, with a fervor that her character, Mayavati, would have admired. "No, Virat. Let's talk about the one thing we've both avoided for long enough. Let's talk about why it's so hard to fathom for your brilliant brain that you're one of only two men I can absolutely trust in this world? That my friendship with your brother has eaten away at you for ten long years?"

"Don't, Zara," he said, a slow fury awakening in his eyes. It etched itself onto his features, and even then, Zara's heart only marveled at how beautiful he was in the moment. How so very breathtaking he was, how deeply he could feel…how much she wanted to hold him and press her face into that warm chest. How much she never wanted to let him go.

"Don't what, Virat?"

"Don't talk about trust as if this was a remotely normal relationship. As if this is anything more than a convenient fling for both of us," he gritted out.

"It started as that, yes, but I was just kidding myself. This is the first relationship I've had in ten years. Ten long years where I didn't lack for interest from men. Good men, even. I've already made my peace with the fact that you're the only man I can let my guard down with. That you're the only one I can let close, even if it's just nothing but a fling.

"And that I can't stand for you to look at me with that same contempt you show the entire world."

"I don't."

"Yes, you do. I told you, Virat. I know you better than anyone else. I know how deeply you feel things. I know you're nothing like the superficial playboy you show the world. I…know you, Virat."

"Leave it alone, Zara."

"I can't. I'd rather you call me the vilest names you can think of to my face than blow hot and cold with me. I can't take it when you look at me as if I'm a stranger to you."

He closed his eyes and looked away. "Because you are."

"No, I'm not." And then Zara asked the question she'd wanted to from the first moment he'd taunted her. "Why do you think I traded you for Vikram, as you called it?"

"Damn it, Zara! Because you did. You built your entire career on the back of your relationship with me, using me to get to him. I tried to…" He pushed his fingers through his hair roughly. "I understand how hard it is to get traction in this industry. I… know that.

I expected that kind of behavior from everyone else. I grew up amid it. But you…" He looked at her then and Zara gasped at the pain etched deep into those familiar features. "I thought the world of you. I…but you simply cashed it all in."

Zara felt his words like a slap. She'd pushed him to this, she'd foolishly wanted to break down the barrier that their past had left between them. She'd wanted more. And yet, his accusation stole the ground from under her. She wished she could simply walk away from this. From him. From the past.

But she couldn't. She wouldn't sleep a wink

or function like a normal human being while he thought the worst of her. She was done fighting the power this man had over her. Done questioning why her heart beat a thousand times louder near him. Why he meant so much to her.

She folded her arms, bracing herself for more. "Is that what you think I did?"

"Please don't pretend. I can forgive you anything except the pretense that you didn't take money from my mother to leave me. And that she didn't pull a number of strings behind the scenes to land you that role with Bhai—the one that launched your career, the one that started your friendship with Bhai, as a bonus payment for leaving me."

Zara had no idea how she managed to stay upright. How she didn't launch herself at him, screaming that it was all lies. Big, fat lies. That there were reasons why she'd left him but they had nothing to do with money or her relationship with Vikram. That Virat was the only man who brought her alive. Who made her take risk after risk with her battered heart. "And you know this how?" she asked calmly, already knowing the answer.

"Mama told me that you'd struck a deal with her. That when she approached you, all you could talk about was how much you'd wanted to land a role in Bhai's movie. How desperate you were that your career wasn't going anywhere..."

She flinched but fired back, "You knew what my career meant to me, Virat. So is it my ambition that you're holding against me? Because, if it is, it makes you worse than all the other men floating around."

"No, *shahzadi*," he said, and Zara wondered if he even realized how he was addressing her. "Don't lay that sin at my feet. You thinking Bhai was a better bet for your career…skewered me, yes. But that was the truth back then. I was nothing and he was everything.

"But what bothers me, as much as I try to get over it, is the fact that you used our relationship to do it, Zara. It was your bargaining chip with my mother. It turned everything into a transaction. It tainted everything we had.

"It was worse than losing you…to him."

"He never had me, Virat. Don't you get that?"

"I know that, Zara. Now. But I was an angry twenty-year-old who thought you were rejecting me for him."

"But that's not true. Don't you understand that there's a reason I found my way back to you again?"

"The resentful bastard in me says it's because I'm me now. A powerful man in his own right."

Zara flopped onto the settee behind her, her knees shaking beneath her. "Wow, so you think I came back to you because now you are of use to me again?"

"No. I don't." He pressed the heels of his palms to his eyes. "You have nothing but my respect, Zara. But the past…" an angry groan fell from his chest "…is like an angry shadow that haunts me."

"Then maybe you've become the very man you've

hated your entire life," Zara said softly. "Maybe you're more like your father than you realize—a man who's so caught up in the past that he ruins his own future."

If she thought he'd mock her that she wasn't part of his future, he didn't. His gaze shifted away from her but not before she saw him flinch. His words when he spoke felt like they were wrenched from him. As if the very thought had haunted him. "You think that possibility hasn't occurred to me? You think I'm not trying every moment to let the past go?"

And that was what these two days of respite had been. Zara knew he was trying to let things be. Knew she had pushed him into that place of hurt and irrationality. Knew that…he'd always tried to live his life guided by those very principles that had drawn him to her.

Frustration raked its nails through her at the specter of past always coming between them. She believed him that he wanted to get past it. But he never might. And that broke her heart a little.

Of course, Vandana Raawal had lied about Zara's reasons for leaving. She'd spun the entire thing to make herself look better to her rebellious son. She had used the opportunity to get closer to the son she'd already hurt beyond repair.

After all, the absolute truth was Vandana had picked Zara's audition tape from hundreds and put it in front of Vikram.

In a twisted world, she could even understand the desperate woman's motivations. After all, when

Vandana had approached Zara, she'd thought she'd been doing the right thing for her son. She had thought Zara wasn't good enough for him.

But for Virat to have believed that Zara had taken money from his mother to leave him, that she'd been out to get everything she could, that their relationship hadn't meant the world to her, that it hadn't nearly broken her to walk away from the one man who'd made her feel alive again…that hurt.

The truth was, she hadn't been ready for another serious relationship after her travesty of a marriage and her husband's death. She didn't even know who she'd been back then.

He came to her then, his long fingers falling on her shoulders gently. Her skin tingled with awareness. Every inch of her body prickled with that mixture of excitement and anticipation. A quiet joy that her mind would always associate with the very scent of this man.

"Zara," he whispered, his breath coating her temple. "I'm not a small man who begrudges you the career you've made for yourself. I…" his jaw tightened "…don't want to be…"

Zara pushed his hands away and stepped back.

She'd vowed to herself a long time ago that no man was ever going to make her feel small again. No man was ever going to control her happiness again. And she couldn't let Virat do it to her, either, she thought bitterly. Even though there was a part of her that now understood how shattered he must have been to think she'd left him for money and to get a role in Vikram's film.

"I'm ever so grateful that you slept with me even though this is what you think of me, Virat. I can't tell you how—"

"Stop, Zara. I've tried to forget the past. I've forgiven you. I realize I was an idealistic prig back then. It doesn't matter what I thought of you, of us. After ten years, I can see it as less of a betrayal and more as a powerless woman using everything she had to get ahead in an industry that rewards connections and power."

"Wow, so you forgive me, do you?" Zara retorted, sheer fury pushing away the hurt that he'd think that of her. "Then let me tell you that you're still an idealistic prig. You… You're right. This was never going to be easy or fun or just a fling." She looked away from him, feeling as if she was saying goodbye to him all over again.

She felt his chin rest on her head, his fingers tightening around her shoulders. Felt his harsh exhale stroke the skin of her neck. She desperately wanted to lean back into his hard body, to let him enfold her in those strong arms.

He was waiting for her to do just that. She knew. Letting her decide the course of this. Letting her know with that voluble silence of his that he still wanted her. That they could just bury the past here in this moment, thorns and all.

That they could continue this thing between them for as long as she pleased. That he wanted her, despite what he thought she might have done. Every inch of her wanted to lean back into him, to cover the distance.

She took a bracing breath instead and said, "I swore to myself a long time ago that I'd never cry again in front of a man. Please leave, Virat."

The sudden cold kissing her spine told her he had left. And now that he was gone, she perversely wanted him back. Wanted him to hold her and kiss her and make love to her until she was too trembling and sated to think straight.

Zara didn't cry. Exhaustion and that same nausea she'd been battling for weeks now began to set in, leaving her body sore and achy. But as she flopped down onto the bed and buried her face in the scent of the man she missed like an ache already, she wondered why she hadn't simply told him the truth. Why she hadn't simply defended herself.

Vandana Raawal had lied to her son. Outright, completely lied that Zara had taken money from her as payment to walk away from Virat. She'd not only convinced Zara that she wasn't good enough for her son, that she was ruining Virat's bright future back then, but she'd also broken her son's heart with her own hands. Ruined his trust in Zara.

Even worse, she'd broken his trust in himself.

But however she looked at it, Zara knew she'd had a hand in it, too. Her inability to trust him back then, her fears about how her last marriage had turned out and her uncertainty about the future—hers and Virat's—had made her run away from him.

Had made her choose the easy way out, convincing herself it was the best thing for them both.

Was she willing to do the same thing again or was it time to finally tell him the truth about her past and about what his mother had done? She fell asleep, pondering the answer to that question, desperately missing Virat in her bed and in her heart.

CHAPTER TEN

ZARA ARRIVED AT the audio release party being held at a sprawling luxury resort, another property that Virat had invested in, her belly full of fluttering butterflies.

Since Virat was flying in at the last minute from God knows where, there hadn't been a need for them to arrive together. Instead, she happily joined Vikram and Naina, even though the both of them kept stealing glances at her face. That she had fainted the other afternoon was news she couldn't have kept to herself.

The only mitigating factor had been that Virat had already left. She'd had a reprieve to deal with everything. Before she had to face him again.

She'd seen him on set for the last week of the shoot, and for the impromptu wrap-up party Vikram had arranged for the team. Thanks to their crazy schedules, she and Virat hadn't had the time or the need to act all lovey-dovey in front of others.

Ten days after their argument, she was less hurt with his impression of her and the past, and more…

angry at herself. Not explaining about her marriage and its aftermath, and then running away from what he'd made her feel the last time around was what had caused all this. She'd opened the door to allow in Vandana's manipulation and lies.

Not that he was without fault. But then, Zara also knew how deep old wounds could run. How they twisted and corrupted everything that was good in life.

She was done running. From him or herself. Especially now.

She was pregnant. With Virat's child.

Nearly six weeks along. And thanks to the intense cardio regimen and sixteen-hour workdays, she'd been completely unaware of the changes in her own body. At least, the lack of hunger and the exhaustion all made sense now.

Three days later, she still couldn't manage her emotions at what her blood test had finally confirmed. Elation sent her swinging high one moment, and then the idea of confronting Virat with the truth sending her mood dipping low the next.

Like a coward, she'd even indulged in the idea of skipping this release party in its entirety. She could have claimed she was feeling unwell and it wouldn't have been a complete lie.

But she also knew she had to face Virat soon. She was wary of his reaction, yes, but this wasn't something she wanted to hide from him. No more evasions, no more lies between them.

No expectations. She kept whispering that as her mantra. Whatever his reaction, she wasn't going to be surprised by it.

The last thing she wanted was to force him into a role he wasn't ready for, to somehow ingratiate herself into his life in this way. But she did want to share it with him first. She wanted to share everything she was feeling, she wanted to…

No, Zara! No expectations, remember?

The audio release was the first in a chain of PR events that were still to come, to build the buzz for the film's release in three months. While the schedule had overwhelmed her, Zara was glad of the extended leave she'd scheduled for herself at the end of the biopic's production.

Today's event also constituted the first look at the stills from the film and a trailer. It had exceeded even the stir that Virat and Vikram had hoped to cause. She couldn't remember the number of people—both familiar and unfamiliar—that she had smiled at, or shaken hands with, or accepted congratulations from. The movie trailer had spurred such an applause from the audience that it was still ringing in her ears.

Even though she'd been present for the last week of filming as Virat had pushed and pushed both Vikram and her to do better, the trailer was still a shock. Her performance, even in the forty-five seconds she had in the trailer, was breath-stealing.

Her gaze had automatically sought his in the darkened auditorium as if tugged toward him.

There was no smile on his lips as he held her gaze. Not after they'd had to embrace and laugh and kiss each other on stage, to please the crowd. Not when within moments of touching, they'd lost themselves in each other.

Not when the possibility of something real and raw danced into life every time their eyes met. When it was clear that for all their arguments, nothing had changed between them.

And yet everything had changed.

Zara sat back into her chair and closed her eyes. Praying to God for composure for just a little longer.

The lights came back on, and onstage, Vikram talked about how the project was a culmination of years of thought and effort—a homage to his grandfather Vijay Raawal. A continuation of the prestigious Raawal legacy.

Zara felt a sudden flush claim her skin and she laid a hand on her still-flat belly. Her child would now also be a part of that legacy. Her child would be...

When Virat arrived on the stage, there was a feverish anticipation in the crowd. And while he thanked his brother for giving him the opportunity to direct such a masterpiece, and said Vijay Raawal was an inspiration to everyone in the film industry, he didn't mention the Raawal family or his place in the legacy at all.

Making Zara wonder yet again how he would take her news after all. Reminding her that she'd tangled with a man who'd always forged his own path.

But before he left the stage, Virat thanked each and every technician and staff member for putting up with him.

Zara clapped the hardest, feeling a profound gratitude and a strange pride in him. As if he belonged to her.

Even now, as she circulated among the glitterati who had been fortunate enough to get the first glimpse of the magnum opus of the Raawal House of Cinema, she couldn't believe what she had seen with her own eyes.

Vikram had always had a magnetic presence on screen, and his portrayal of his grandfather had been truly sensational. But she…she had shone. Virat had been absolutely right—it was her chance to steal the scene from her leading man and she had done it. In just a matter of a few weeks, she felt as if she had learned a lifetime's worth of skills under Virat's direction.

The man was truly a genius behind the camera at what he could wring out of the actors on the screen. And in real life, he was a man who'd built an island around himself. A man who used the camera as a shield between himself and the world.

Picking up a glass of sparkling water from a passing waiter, she drank it in one go, hoping it would settle her stomach. It was more than three hours now and all she wanted was to take Virat's hand and disappear.

As if summoned, he was there on the next blink. She felt him at her back, the warmth of his wiry body beckoning her closer. The hair on the nape of her neck prickled with awareness.

"You fainted as soon as I left? Did you miss me that much, *shahzadi*?" His words were a raspy whisper against the rim of her ear.

Zara knew he was teasing her and yet the truth of that thought struck her still.

She felt him lean down. His fingers landed gently on her shoulders and squeezed, even as a photographer captured them from the other side. Neither did she miss the curious glances, from family members and friends to the press and other media moguls.

Zara gritted her teeth against the self-indulgent anger that rose through her. She was beginning to hate the very charade she'd started. She wanted his raw intensity, the real man, and not this polite, attentive lover he played in front of the world.

When he'd have retreated, Zara kept her hand clasped around his neck.

"More posturing, *shahzadi*? If I'm to hold you and kiss you and touch you for public consumption, then I'm going to demand the same in private," he whispered, bending down to rub his unshaven cheek against hers.

She looked into his eyes, the naked want in his tone finding an echo in her. "Don't mock this.

Whatever you might think of the past, if you mock what I feel for you…"

He raised his hands, palms up. "No mockery, Zara. The entire world be damned, I refuse to continue this charade in public and then go to my bed alone. I want you, *shahzadi.* I can't sleep without you by my side. I admit that I want to see where this will take us."

Excitement thumped so hard in her chest that it filled her ears. She desperately wanted to take what he was offering. Especially now. If she weren't pregnant, if she were free to take risk after risk…

"Are you going to practice forgiveness afresh every morning then?" Zara couldn't help taunting back.

Deep grooves formed around his mouth as he considered her. "I've never said I was perfect, Zara. But I'm trying to let things be."

Zara shook her head, wondering why she was pushing this again. When there were bigger, life-changing matters waiting ahead for them to discuss. "I've already done the whole vicious cycle of having a man heap abuse on me the previous night and then pledge a fresh start the next morning, in my last marriage. For three long years. By the end of it, I was completely twisted up, inside out. I lost myself."

Stillness enveloped him, and when he spoke, shock pervaded his every word. "Really, Zara, now? You choose to tell me this now?"

Zara regretted the words instantly. It was as if there was no filter left anymore within her. "That was a cheap shot." She held onto him when he'd have stepped back. "I'm sorry. It was unfair to compare you to...him. I... I don't want to do this, Virat. I don't want this to be our default setting."

His forearm came around her back and he held her so gently that for the first time in years, Zara thought she might break. "No, Zara. Don't apologize."

A sudden shiver took over her body. "I don't want this poison to fester, Virat. Not between you and me. I can't stand the thought of that. Whatever the future holds, I don't want us to part like this."

"Shh...*shahzadi*. Shh... Nothing like that is going to happen to us. I've got you, Zara. I'm... so—"

The last thing Zara wanted from him was an apology. Not like this. Never like this.

Throwing every warning to the wind, she snuck her fingers into his hair and pulled him down until his mouth met hers. She was hungry for him, for his warmth, for his kiss, for the strength of his arms around her. She felt his shock for maybe a second.

Then he took the kiss over, and every muscle in Zara's body sighed in shuddering relief. It felt like coming home after years and years of being away.

He explored her mouth with a wondrous gentleness that brought tears to her eyes. This was no rough possession. This felt like escape and invitation, all blended together into a soft storm. Like a new beginning between them, washing away the pain of the past.

This felt like retreating into a world in which only they both existed. He kissed her as if he had been waiting for her to make the move again. Even as she drowned in the warm cavern of his mouth, Zara couldn't help but demand more. Want more.

"I'm not going to apologize for doing that," she whispered against his cheek, keeping her fingers in his hair. "Nor am I going to pretend that it was for someone else's benefit."

He raised a brow, challenge glinting in his eyes. "No?"

"No. I needed that kiss."

He laughed, sending vibrations into her mouth and the rest of her body. She tightened her fingers in his hair, punishing him for the taunt. Desperate for the anchoring of his taste, she clung to him, her breaths suddenly shallow.

His fingers gently clasped her face as he studied her. "Something's bothering you, Zara. You're not yourself."

She looked into his eyes and there was no laughter there. He knew. Just like that. Rubbing a finger over her lips, she nodded. "We need to talk. I've been waiting for you to get back."

He frowned, his gaze studying her intently. "We'll leave immediately." He pushed onto his feet and took her hand in his. "Are you unwell?"

"Yes. No. I mean, I know why I haven't been feeling completely okay."

Her statement shocked him, she knew. But his expression remained steady. And that was what

Zara needed. "I have a suite on the thirty-fifth floor. We'll talk there."

Zara looked around and noted that their departure was already making waves. "Vikram will kill me for dragging you away," she muttered.

"Bhai knows this is not where I naturally shine, Zara. This is his arena."

When she still looked doubtful, he wrapped his arm around her waist and pulled her. "Come, *shahzadi.* Your career won't sink if you bunk off being on show for one evening."

It felt as if it took no longer than a blink of an eye before the lift pinged and they were walking through the white marbled foyer into the sitting lounge. Beautiful teak furnishings gave the room a warm glow. Greenery draped from ceilings and climbed along the white walls, giving the expansive space a very cozy feel.

Zara knew Virat was watching her. Waiting for her to speak. And that she was only postponing the inevitable. She took a bracing breath and turned around.

He'd already thrown his jacket away and undone the cuffs of his linen shirt. Dark and broad and unfailingly male, he made Zara's pulse dance in her chest. She swallowed and looked away.

He came close and whispered her name, a thousand questions in it. "Zara?"

Zara looked at him, and blurted it out. "I'm pregnant. I'm about six weeks along." She had to take a long breath at the end of that statement. And when he didn't move or even blink, she whispered inanely, "It's yours, Virat. The baby's yours."

* * *

Virat laughed. Or at least he'd thought he'd laughed. But the sound that emerged was a hollow, lackluster mockery of the real thing. "I didn't think otherwise, Zara. But thank you for the clarification."

"Oh, I didn't mean to say that you doubted me. I'm sorry I have no template for how to do this and I shouldn't have just blurted it out like that—"

"Don't. God. Please stop apologizing." He pressed a hand to his temple and let out another laugh. "There's no speech you could give that could prepare me for that revelation, is there? So yeah, don't worry about your delivery."

She didn't move. Just looked at him steadily. Ever the poised woman. As if waiting patiently to let him process it all.

For a few seconds, he wondered if he was in some sort of a strange feverish dream he usually had when he was sleep-deprived. When the rest and peace he desperately wanted eluded him.

But that wasn't possible. Because he didn't want to tie himself down to Zara, did he? Not when he still didn't completely trust her, when he didn't like that she continued to haunt his every waking thought.

Not when she was beginning to matter too much.

No. The last thing he should want, or dream about, was that Zara was pregnant with his child. With *his* child.

A girl or a boy who might look up to him. A totally innocent child who would be affected by his every word, gesture or action. Or by the very lack of word, gesture or action from him.

Virat thought he might throw up without the benefit of alcohol for the first time in his life.

"Virat?" Zara asked, her eyes wide, her stance both challenging and yet defensive. As if she was ready for anything he might throw at her. When it was she who'd been turning his life upside down from the minute she'd walked back into it.

"You're determined to pull me under, aren't you, *shahzadi*?" he asked then. The words came automatically, as if his brain could send mechanical responses while his heart...his heart tackled the avalanche of emotions that threatened to drown him. If he let them...

"Pull you under?" she said, coming closer tentatively.

"First you blurt out to me that you...that your marriage was a..." He rubbed his hand over his face, unable to even form the words. The outrage that filled him at the pain he'd seen in her eyes defied words.

God, he'd been so blind. The signs of an abusive marriage had all been there. When they'd met back then, she'd been so wary of him in the beginning. Of any man who might have been even a little friendly. Constantly on alert as if she was afraid he might steal something she didn't want to give. Needlessly second-guessing her every small decision.

Her wonder at the silliest of sights. Her sudden alertness as if someone might have been watching and gauging her every word and action. The silent tears she'd cried when he'd taken her on a tour of the city at night.

And now, after all these years, the simple admission that she hadn't taken a lover in ten years. That she couldn't let her guard down with anyone else. With any other man but him. He considered himself a good judge of human character, a master of human nature, and yet he'd been so blind to it.

"Virat… I shouldn't have mentioned it at all. Not like that and not tonight of all nights."

"You should have told me a long time ago, *shahzadi*," he added, and regretted the demanding words immediately. The last thing he wanted was to heap more accusations on her, to make this all about him. "Zara, the last thing I want is to hurt you. Even before you told me about this. That's why I made myself stay away."

"I know that. I do. It's just that if I had told you about what a disaster my first marriage had been, how long it has taken me to gain my confidence back, you'd look at me as you're doing now. As if you had to weigh every word you say to me. As if I was nothing more than a victim." Frustration painted her face. "I've earned the right to be seen as more than a sum of my past. Don't take that away from me now, Virat. I couldn't bear it if you… looked at me like that."

"No one can take that away from you, Zara." He understood her perfectly in that moment. And all he felt was that same inadequacy that had haunted him since she'd asked him to leave the bedroom ten days ago. He chose his words carefully. "I won't ask you to talk about it," he said. "Not tonight. Not ever if you don't want to. But, Zara, I would like to know. When you're ready. When you think I've earned the right to share that episode of your life."

"Yes, okay," she said, clearly eager to get away from the subject. "Now can we talk about the…baby?"

He pushed a hand through his hair, a knot of uncomfortable sensations sitting like a damned weight on his chest. God, there was so much to unpack, so much waiting to drown him. But the wariness in her eyes gave him the anchor he needed right now.

This wasn't about him or the ground being pulled away from under him, or whether he wanted to be a father or not. This was about Zara and what she needed from him now. What she wanted from him. And that was what he should focus on.

He went to her then and took her hand in his. Gently squeezed the long fingers. There was still a fragility about the fine angles of her face but also a quiet spark of resolve that made him relax. Clearly, she was handling this better than him. "You have decided to keep the baby, haven't you?"

"Yes, I have." She sighed. "I've never thought of myself as a mother but…it's strange how right it felt once it sank in. If there's one thing I've learned, it's that life never works out the way we expect.

"I met Saleem at a wedding and fell in love overnight. I went against my parents' warnings that we were too young and married him. I had so many plans for my life with him. And then…a few days into our married life, he changed. He refused to let me pursue acting. Even though he knew it was my passion. He…knocked my confidence in everything.

"Since he passed, I've learned to count my blessings as they come to me, Virat. Ten years ago, it was meeting you in line for coffee.

"Now, it's this chance to be a mother when I didn't even plan for it.

"I choose to see this as a good thing. Can you understand that?"

There was such sheer confidence and joy in her words that Virat had no words, for a few seconds. And he knew without doubt that his child was indeed fortunate. That Zara would be a wonderful mother.

And the clarity of her vision began to clear his own doubts.

"How do you feel?"

She smiled. "Good. Now that I know the reason for the strange headaches and the lethargy, really relieved. I… I've never fainted before in my life and it took everything I had to get Vikram and Naina to leave me alone so that I could talk to the doctor."

"And she said everything…with the…" he cleared his throat "…baby is good?"

That smile in her eyes again. "Yes. In excellent health. I…" she sighed "…I told her I'd never missed the pill, not one single day. But I did do a round of antibiotics when I caught something while I was traveling just before Vikram's wedding, and she said…"

He cupped her cheek. "You don't owe me an explanation as to why or how it happened, Zara."

"I know. It's just that I've known for three days, and there's so much to talk about…and I was worried that we'd left things in such a bad place. But I…" Her hesitation made his rollicking thoughts come to a halt.

"What, Zara? Tell me what you're thinking."

"I'm glad…you see that this is my decision. I'm the one taking on this responsibility and…you don't have to…" Virat didn't know what she saw in his face because that wariness came back again. "I want to make it clear that there's no pressure on you at all. You…you can decide how much of a role you want to play in the child's life. You can…"

Virat stood up, a restless energy crawling under his skin. A strange anger was coiling around his limbs and he didn't even understand at what, or why.

He looked out into the night, his emotions just as dark and unruly. All his life, he'd possessed a thorough awareness of his dreams and fears. Even as a child, he'd had to develop the sort of emotional intelligence to deal with his father's cold distance.

And yet, suddenly it felt as if he didn't know himself at all. As if there was a hungry cavern inside of him that wanted what it wanted. "I don't want any child of mine to go through what I did. I don't want him or her to ever doubt its roots, its family, its very existence. That's nonnegotiable, Zara."

"Of course. I wouldn't dream of denying our child that knowledge. Or you of whatever relationship you wanted with her or him.

"You know what calmed me down when the magnitude of this hit me? When I thought, *Oh, my*

God, I'm going to be a mother and I don't know the first thing about it?"

"What?"

He felt her move behind him. Her arms came around his waist, as if she knew that the calm persona he was showing her right now was nothing but a facade. Her breasts pressed up against his back, her cheek against his shoulder, she draped herself all over him.

"You…the thought of *you* calmed me down. That whatever way we do this, however I bring up this child, our child, that I will have your support in every decision. That…we will somehow muddle through this together."

He scoffed. "You have a lot more trust in me than I do in myself right now, *shahzadi*. I know next to nothing about bringing up a child."

She laughed then and he felt the vibrations of her laughter sink into his skin. And Virat knew, in that moment, that this was his chance to do it right. His chance to build everything he'd been denied his entire life. "Neither do I. And what I have trust in is *us* together. I trust that whatever the past, and the future, we both will always want and do the best for this baby."

He turned and took her mouth in a kiss that was more necessary than breath itself. She moaned into his mouth, just as eager as him, cementing the decision that was gaining momentum inside him.

He wrapped an arm around her waist and pulled her closer. The other hand, he sent on a foray, needing the feel of her soft curves to calm the furor in his blood. The more he touched her and kissed her, the more Virat felt the rightness of his decision.

He pulled away and leaned his forehead against hers, his breaths just as shallow as hers.

"Shall I tell you what I want, then, Zara? How I want this to play out?"

"Yes," she whispered. "I just don't want any more shadows between us, Virat. No more things that can fester."

"A fresh start, then, *shahzadi*?"

She smiled, and her face lit up with a glorious kind of joy. "Yes, exactly. We will start a new scene. Draw a line under the past."

"Then let's turn our engagement into the real thing. Let's get married."

She jerked away from him, just as he'd expected. But Virat didn't release his hold on her. She was soft and solid and real in his arms—more real than anything he'd ever beheld in his life. "What?"

Virat led with logic, knowing that that was the only way to appeal to Zara. "We're knee-deep in an engagement that will continue for at least another three months. At least until the release of the biopic, is what we said, right? And by then… I assume you're going to be showing."

"Yes," she said, her eyes full of that wariness. "But—"

"Do you want to split up then, Zara? Do you want to put yourself through the stress of going through a separation that's splashed all over the press? Do you want me to play the role of the heartless bastard who dumped his pregnant fiancée?

"Do you want to start our future together as parents like that?"

"But—"

"Or do you want to start as a married couple who want to do the right thing by their child? A couple who know exactly what to expect from each other? Is there a better foundation to begin our life together?"

"And you won't care about giving up your bachelorhood? Tying yourself to me permanently?"

"Like you said, we're already tied together, Zara. This baby has already changed everything. I'm just streamlining the process and trying to make everything official."

She laughed and he held her close, and Virat knew that this was the right thing to do. For the first time in years, he felt a strange sort of peace fill him. And he didn't worry over how easy and effortless this felt. How…right it felt.

But then, as he'd learned in the last ten years, when it came to his personal life, decisions made with his head rather than his heart, always worked out.

And maybe that made him a fraud, but he knew that life was nowhere near as logical or neat or even sane, as the most chaotic piece of it captured as a piece of art.

CHAPTER ELEVEN

ZARA HAD NEVER imagined planning the wedding—especially her wedding—could be this much fun. Of course, this time she wasn't planning to run away with a man she barely knew, against her parents' wishes. Wasn't young and impulsive and looking for a way out of her mundane life.

It also helped that she had the wealth this time to properly plan the wedding. Even though she'd had to naysay her groom again and again when he insisted that first she let him pay, and second, she pick a wedding planner and take it easy.

She'd commissioned Anya Raawal to create a custom-designed *lehenga* and a sari for the two ceremonies, and the brilliant girl had accepted, her gaze bright with joy. Anya had simply said, "He seems so happy, Ms. Khan. I've never seen my brother like that."

Of course, Zara had immediately told her to call her Bhaabi, like she did Naina.

It didn't matter that what she was planning was for a small, intimate wedding of no more than ten that constituted her closest family and friends. And even in that, half of the guest list comprised the Raawal family. The thought of coming face-to-face with Vandana Raawal had made her more than a little anxious, but Zara had decided that Vandana was unlikely to confess to Virat what she'd done to him ten years ago, and that nothing, not even her deceitful future mother-in-law and her obsession with her younger son, was going to mar the pleasure she was discovering in all the details that were going into planning two different ceremonies.

Her mother had been quite insistent that Zara should have a proper *nikaah* this time, and Zara had heartily agreed. In a twist that even she hadn't seen coming, Virat had, of course, charmed the pants off her strict English teacher mother by visiting her without Zara's knowledge. "He didn't say he was going to make you happy, Zara. He knows you well, *beta*. He simply said he'd do his best to keep up with my powerhouse daughter." Zara had closed her eyes, fighting the tears that threatened to overflow. The man did know her well. Her mother's fluttery "He's so…handsome and…sexy, Zara," at the end of the phone call had sent her into paroxysms of laughter.

"You've chosen well, *beta*," she had added softly. And Zara's heart had felt full to bursting. "He seems like a very thoughtful young man."

It had been a month since their fake engagement had turned into a real one. The night he'd proposed, Virat had simply asked her to consider his proposal without rejecting it outright. Had stayed with her all night long and made love to her in such a tender, gentle way that she'd ended up crying in his arms.

She'd woken up in the early hours of the morning to find his palm on her belly and a sort of wonder etched into his face. His gaze had been somewhere else, until Zara had clasped his cheek and kissed him. She'd seen something there, then—a wretched sort of loneliness that she understood very well.

"Whatever you decide, Zara, we'll be a family. Of our own making."

She had nodded and demanded that he hold her. Desperate to have him back, away from the shadows of the painful past that glimmered in his face. And she'd known then that she'd already made her decision.

Happiness was a choice, and Zara wanted to spend the rest of her life building on the magic that was already there between them. Not that Virat had taken her acceptance for granted.

No, he'd waged a weeklong seduction campaign that Zara had been all too happy to succumb to. If he wasn't bringing her her favorite desserts from all around the world, he was bringing her old gramophone records of artists from a long-gone era. He'd cooked for her, gone over possible scripts with her that she might consider in the future, and found new and adventurous ways to make love to her.

Just thinking of the last time he had taken her to bed sent heat flushing through Zara. What had begun as an innocent massage of her feet when she'd complained of exhaustion had somehow turned into the wicked man going on his knees in front of the sofa where she'd been sitting, and burying his face between her thighs.

Zara still had no idea how he made sex so raw and intimate.

How one night, they'd communicate with greedy fingers and throaty gasps and the damp slide of their bodies in the darkness. And the next, they would be watching some cheesy movie in bed for research, laughing, taunting each other. And amid that laughter he would strip her and slowly slide into her ready heat, and her laughter would transform into desperate need.

One evening, she'd opened a safe sex box from one of the rural outreach projects she was overseeing, and out had popped a tube of lube. Of course, the wicked man had immediately suggested they test the product and they'd lost track of time and had arrived flushed and late to a dinner with Vikram and Naina.

If she'd been hovering over the threshold before, now she was completely, irrevocably in love with him. She loved how he didn't hesitate to discuss their future. How he bossed her around when he thought she was unnecessarily tiring herself.

How he spoiled her rotten when the mood took him. How he could go from demanding and insatiable to a gentle lover who wanted nothing more than to hold her through the night.

"I'm so happy for you both, Zara," Naina had said, when Zara had informed them that the wedding was imminent. Vikram had looked relieved and hugged Zara so tight for so long that Virat had growled and pulled her away. Leaving Naina in a fit of giggles at his jealous behavior.

Zara had felt a strange reluctance to share the news of their pregnancy, even with her best friend and his wife. And Virat had understood her reluctance without her having to spell it out. Only then did Zara realize that he was a very private man. Especially when it came to things that mattered the most to him.

That even with his brother—with whom he shared a true bond despite their creative differences and career trajectories—there was a shield he maintained. As if he didn't dare let anyone close. As if he'd become an island so that no one could hurt him.

And yet he'd let her in, Zara knew. He'd let her see the true Virat, despite what he thought she'd done to him. The man who loved and hurt and felt things so deeply.

Despite that, she didn't have a single doubt in her head that her pregnancy was the primary reason he had proposed marriage. She did want her child to know her father, but sometimes she woke up in the middle of the night feeling as if she had lost him once again, and reached for him.

His bare back warm to her touch, his muscles solid and real, he was always there. She blinked at the realization that in the weeks since they had been engaged—the real engagement—he'd spent almost every evening with her. It was as if he had decided, just as she had, that he was going to give this everything.

When Zara had asked him if they should have the wedding the morning before the release of the movie, he had sent her an almost forbidding look. Not that it scared her one bit.

"Don't glare at me," she'd said, wrapping her arms around him and pressing her cheek to his chest. Outside of having him inside her, making sweet love to her, this was Zara's favorite thing to do. She'd realized he wasn't given to overt displays of affection but she didn't care. He was big and solid and hers, and she had already spent so many years denying what she felt for him, battling loneliness. The thud of his heart against her ear made her feel safe and warm and alive. "It's an option I'm exploring, that's all," she'd said, pressing her finger to the ferocious scowl he wore. "Your schedule is crazy bonkers and that's one of the days where everyone is available and—"

"I don't care if it ends up being just you and me, Zara. And your mother, of course. I don't want to face your mother's wrath if she can't attend." His sudden grin and warmth reminded her of when she'd met him for the first time. "But I don't want even a hint of PR spin about our wedding. If Bhai tries to convince you that the idea of us appearing as a married couple on the eve of the premiere after some top secret, romantic wedding that morning—*because we just couldn't wait*," he said in a mocking, high voice, "will skyrocket the ratings for the movie and create even more interest, then I'll throw the punch that he deserved to get the other night at dinner when he kept hugging you."

Zara's mouth twitched and his scowl turned into an outright glower. "Let's not get crazy, darling," she said, pressing her lips to his. "That's the last thing we need when the tale of our supposedly twisted love triangle has finally died down. I'll tell your brother that he's not invited to the wedding, how about that?"

"Are you managing me, *shahzadi*?" he'd said then, his eyes blazing with mock severity.

"Manage the most brilliant director of our generation? Me, I wouldn't dare," she'd said, going on her toes, ruffling his hair. She undid the tie he'd just spent ages putting on and slid her greedy hands under his shirt to find the warm, smooth skin of his pecs. She kissed him again, deep and long, uncaring what they'd been talking about, and he let her, knowing very well that she was trying to do exactly that.

It was quite a while before both of them made their way back to the discussion at hand. He looked rumpled from her kisses and Zara decided she liked him like that best.

"I want our marriage, our child, our lives, our entire future," he said, putting on his Italian handmade shoes, "to be separate from the lives we lead on-screen. No performances for the media.

"No public avowals of affection. No discussing our private lives in front of the camera for someone else's titillation. Not even for one of your numerous charity projects and empowerment efforts or anything else. Not even in front of Bhai and my mother will we talk about our life together." He finally looked up. "Is that clear, Zara?"

Zara had simply nodded, knowing where the words were coming from. "I understand, Virat."

"I don't want to have to send our child away to boarding school at some far-off destination, but if that's what it takes to keep the drama of our public lives away from him or her, we will do it. I can't stand the idea of anything or anyone hurting the… baby, even through words."

Zara had gone to him then and hugged him tight, letting him know that she understood perfectly. That he could dictate to her about this until the end of time and she would only agree with him. That their life together would be real and have none of the glittering artificiality his parents had embraced.

He'd simply nodded and left. And for a few seconds, Zara had wondered at the deep wounds still pulsing below the surface of the man he showed the world. At the shadows she saw in his eyes whenever the subject of the Raawals came up. And wished so hard that she hadn't played a part—even unwittingly—in transforming him from that spontaneous, full-of-life twenty-year-old into this hard man who refused to look into his own heart.

And the fact that she was irrevocably in love with even this incarnation of him was simply a fact she was going to have to get used to.

* * *

She had just finished talking to her mom on the phone when Virat walked into their sunroom where she had been lounging about, taste-testing different samples of desserts a caterer had sent her to pick from.

She was definitely going to have to order the *gulab jamun* for their reception. The syrupy, gooey goodness had melted on her tongue. "Will you be mad at me if I tell the caterer you've demanded to taste the *gulab jamun* before we put in an order and then I eat all of your share when they come in?" she said, wiping her fingers on a napkin and looking up.

It only took one look at his face to know something was very wrong. A prickle of nervous apprehension ran down her spine.

"What is it, Virat? What's happened?" She said, looking up from the cozy armchair where she'd been reclining and watching a rerun of an old movie.

He didn't answer her but paced the expansive room, a restless energy radiating from him.

For a few seconds, Zara simply took in how the afternoon sun kissed the rigid line of his jaw, lovingly traced the breath of his wide shoulders. The dark denim clung to his hips and buttocks, and she had to swallow the instant need to touch him, claiming him for herself.

"You said no more lies, Zara."

She jerked her gaze to his and the fury she saw there sent a tendril of fear to blossom in her belly.

"I didn't even know you were back in town," she said, buying for time. "I thought you were flying in tomorrow morning."

He shook his head, seeing through her ploy. "Don't play games with me, Zara."

"I am not," she said defensively.

He sighed and sat down on the armchair far away from where she was sitting. Zara hated the distance he was imposing between them. And knew he'd done it on purpose. For all the control he exerted on himself, Virat's fury was something to see.

He buried his face in his hands, and a long, harsh groan escaped his mouth. Though the sound was muffled by his hands, Zara heard the anger and frustration in it. It made her want to hold him, more than anything else, but she also knew he didn't want to be touched right now. His body language made that much clear.

"I wanted to surprise you tonight, with an engagement party." He checked the time on the Rolex she'd bought him not two weeks ago, and rubbed his face again.

"Your mother's supposed be flying in in an hour. Bhai was going to bring her to my grandmother's house. Naina helped me plan it."

Zara stared blankly, having had no idea about it. She leaped up from the chair and reached him, laughing. She thought she might burst with joy.

But something in his gaze stopped her at the last moment, just as she was about to touch him. Something so hard and flat and so resigned that her heart kicked in her chest.

"I invited my mother and father, too. What you said the last time we talked…about our child growing up as a part of a family, it stayed with me. Despite all the drama my parents created, my grandparents and Bhai and Anya saved me. They… kept me sane and going. I wanted that future for our child.

"So I decided, in that magnanimous way of mine—" his laugh was full of scorn "—to at least try and forget the past, even if I couldn't completely forgive it. I decided that it didn't matter if my mother had a hand in you leaving me. If my father continued to reject me as his son to his dying breath.

"I was a Raawal in all the ways that mattered. So I'd give my child the pride and belonging I had always deserved but was denied. I'd start a fresh slate with my mother, too. She was, of course, overjoyed and couldn't stop singing your praises all morning.

"Then she announced—in that melodramatic way of hers—that admitting to all her sins would absolve her and my father of years of dysfunctional parenting. Would undo all the damage they'd wrought on Bhai and me and Anya."

Zara felt as if a lead weight was sitting on her chest. She knew now where this was going. Her stomach turned over.

"As part of this new awareness," Virat continued, his tone dripping with contempt, "she told me that she had lied to me ten years ago. About you. That she had driven you away. Because, of course, in her twisted mind, driving away the only woman who saw me for who I was, the woman who made me see myself in a new light, was an act of motherly love. Because, in her opinion, you weren't the right woman for me.

"Because she was looking out for me. Because she wanted me to have a wonderful future. Forget all the early childhood trauma she put me through by staying with a man who continually rejected his own child."

"Virat, please listen to me—"

"Apparently, she got rid of a pesky brother-in-law for you, who was determined to prove you were a murderer."

Zara felt as if she was caught in a nightmare of her own making. "Saleem, my first husband, killed himself after I finally worked up the courage to tell him I was leaving him. His controlling behavior had spiraled until he was locking me in my room and refusing to let me out. Yet his younger brother decided I was responsible for his brother's death and was going all out to punish me for it, even if he had to lie to do it.

"Your mother offered to use her power and reach to make the case he was going to lodge against me disappear. I knew that if any of it came out in the press, the chance of me pursuing a career in acting and landing decent roles with that sullied reputation would be nil. And if Saleem's brother had his way, I might even have ended up in prison.

"So yes, I accepted her help. But I thought it had been offered in good faith! I didn't know that she was going to lie to you about it, make me out to be the villain."

He still didn't look at her. His head was cradled in his hands, and Zara knew that she had hurt him again. By hiding this.

"Why didn't you tell me any of this before?"

"Because you were only twenty and bright and brilliant and had your entire future ahead of you..." Her voice broke but Zara continued, "You have to realize that I was a widow, newly out of an abusive marriage, afraid of her own shadow, guilty about the freedom I suddenly had and facing a possible murder charge. What kind of future would you have had with me? I didn't want to drag you down with me, Virat, if it all went wrong."

"You were the first real thing in my life. You stood outside of my prestigious family. Outside of the industry I was surrounded by. Our relationship was something I had chosen for myself."

"And that very intensity of your emotions...that terrified me so much." Zara knelt in front of him, her hands on his knees, her head bent. "It wasn't you that I didn't trust, Virat.

"It was me. I was petrified of how you made me feel, frightened that someone would find out, terrified that you would see who I really was."

"And what would that have been?"

"Nothing. I thought I was nothing. An imposter not worthy of your attention. All I had were empty dreams. Three years with Saleem had dented my confidence in myself, in my decisions. His death damaged my ability to even trust myself, and then his brother accused me of killing him.

"I was already worrying about where we were going, Virat. It felt like we were getting way ahead of ourselves. You even started talking of maybe leaving the industry behind, of starting fresh somewhere else, in a new country. And I… I was scared of leaving you but also terrified of leaving behind everything that was familiar.

"So when your mother approached me and asked me where I saw our affair going, pointed out that I was no good for you, I let her convince me that you were better off without me. That you were just infatuated with me, and if I left, you'd quickly get over me. I let her use her influence to stop Saleem's brother from pursuing the case against me.

"But I thought she was trying to help me. I promise you I didn't cash in on our relationship. I simply walked away from you. When the screen test for it landed in my lap, it was completely coincidental, but I took it as a sign. That I was better off with a career than with a man who deserved so much more than I could ever give him."

Virat looked up and Zara thought she might break into a thousand pieces if he didn't take her into his arms. "Then why lie to me when I blamed you for her actions? Why not tell me the truth then, Zara? God, you know how much I hate lies."

Zara sat back on her heels, guilt clawing at her. How had she made such a bad judgment call? "Because more than anything, I didn't want to hurt you any more by revealing her actions. I knew your relationship with her was already shaky. And I admit that I struggled to tell you what a coward I'd been back then."

He didn't open his eyes and Zara pushed herself between his legs and took his face in her hands. She put every ounce of feeling into her words, trembling with the need to tell him. The words came easily, fluttering onto her lips as if waiting to be released. "Because despite believing the worst of me, you still came back to me.

"You…gave me a chance. You tried to forgive me even when you thought I'd been paid off by your mother. You needed me just as much as I did you. And that, more than anything, convinced me that you and I belong together. This time, I have the guts to stand here and admit that—"

He looked into her eyes then. And the blankness she saw there made her chest hurt. "Don't, Zara."

"I'm in love with you. You make me laugh. I feel…alive even when I'm fighting with you and you pass out one of your dictates. Every time I reached out to you, you've given me more than I could ever ask." She took his hand and placed it on her belly. "Including this baby that neither of us expected."

"Zara—"

But she didn't stop. She wanted to give words to the wonder in her chest. "I have never stopped loving you. Even ten years ago, when you swept me off my feet. Yes, I was scared, but you also made me see myself in a new light. You…made me laugh and find joy in new things. Ultimately, you…helped me heal, even though I didn't realize it until it was too late.

"And now, I'm so much stronger. I love you and I know I can stand by your side and weather anything. As long as we're together—"

He recoiled. "No, Zara, stop." He pushed onto his feet and moved away from her, as if he couldn't bear to be near her. "I can't do this. I'm sorry. I thought I could. But I can't."

The emptiness she'd always been so scared of came barreling at her, and still, Zara tried to hold it off. "You can't do what? Marry me? Build the family that we both want? We've already agreed to draw a line under the past, so at least, look at me and tell me why."

He turned and there was such raw anguish in his eyes that she flinched. Any other man would have given in to the emotions radiating from him. But not Virat. Not when he had had to harden himself against pain and hurt, again and again. "I proposed we get married because I wanted my child to have everything I didn't. Because I thought we both knew what to expect from each other. But… love, Zara…it complicates everything. I didn't sign up for that.

"My mother and father ruined each other's lives and ours in a futile pursuit of love."

"We're not them, Virat," Zara said, trying not to lose patience. Lose hope. "Don't you still get that? We went through the worst, we avoided each other for a decade but we found our way back to each other." She laughed and the sound was a little broken. "I have no expectations of you today that I didn't have yesterday. Nothing has changed."

He pressed a hand to his temple. As if he couldn't take any more. As if hearing her say she loved him was his worst nightmare. "Everything has changed. Your love…if I accept it, will only make me weak. It will suck me in and then…when it's taken away again…"

"It will not be. I'll never stop loving you. Trust this, please. Trust me," she said, reaching out with her hands. Beseeching him to forgive her truly this time. To want her just one more time. To choose her one more time.

Instead, he walked away, leaving Zara standing there alone.

CHAPTER TWELVE

ZARA ARRIVED AT the first premiere of the biopic to a select audience of critics and industry pundits after two months on an uncommonly cold spring night in an off-white, sleeveless silk blouse and a beautiful handwoven silk sari in the same white shade, with a beautiful red border in contrast. The best part, however, had been that the sari had come pre-stitched—as if the designer had known that a four-and-a-half-months pregnant woman would have to manage it. So all Zara had had to do was to pull it on and one of her friends, Anna—who had sung the soundtrack for the movie—had easily pinned it over Zara's shoulder.

Her hair had been braided and dressed in a beautiful knot, and a white jasmine *gajra* wound around the knot.

The PR person had delivered, along with the sari and the blouse, a heavy pearl necklace intertwined with shimmering rubies in an antique Hyderabadi design and matching *jhumkas*. She knew the color scheme would be coordinated with Vikram's clothes as they were appearing together at the premiere and at the after-party tonight.

Zara had always loved the simple and stunning beauty of a sari. But this sari—so close in shade and texture to the one she'd picked for her and Virat's Hindu wedding ceremony, draped beautifully, even around her rounding belly. It felt as if it was made of clouds, and floated with Zara as she moved.

For a few seconds after Anna had left, Zara had stood staring at herself in the full-length mirror in her bedroom.

Until today, Zara had worn mostly loose, free-flowing dresses at the few PR events she'd attended. With her statuesque frame and long legs, it had been very easy to hide her pregnancy. Even though it had been Virat who had decided it, Zara had also loathed the very idea of talking about their relationship or the pregnancy or anything else to the press.

Only Mama, Naina and her friend Anna knew about the baby, because when Zara had told them they were postponing the wedding date, they'd all simply showed up one evening demanding to know everything and wouldn't leave until she'd told them at least part of it.

The whole truth about what had happened felt intimate and private and something that only belonged to both her and Virat. Since she'd had a scheduled vacation anyway, she'd mostly laid low.

Tonight would be her first public appearance with her small belly showing clearly. She knew it was going to create more than just waves. But she wasn't going to hide it anymore, either.

Their relationship, it seemed, was in limbo.

Virat hadn't announced to the world that he had dumped his pregnant fiancée because she had admitted she was in love with him. And Zara had left it alone, too. She wasn't the one who'd walked away. If he wanted to tell the world that they were done, then he was welcome to do it himself.

At first, she'd been so unbelievably crushed that if not for her mother's opportune arrival for the blasted party that Virat had arranged, she would have walked around her bungalow like some ghostly apparition singing mournfully about the true love who'd deserted her for a richer, prettier woman.

Like the very scene she loved so much from a slapstick comedy/thriller Virat had written and directed a few years ago. The shimmering ghost woman, turns out to have killed her lover before the movie begins, and in a brilliant reversal, it is the man that turns out to be the ghost.

With its masterful visual effects and immersive storytelling, the movie was an ode to his talent.

As her chauffeur maneuvered the Mercedes around the bustling square and traffic to the newly renovated centuries-old theater—where Vijay Raawal had released his first movie years ago, Zara had a flash of complete empathy with the heroine of Virat's movie.

She would have very much liked to bash his stubborn head against something hard until he saw sense. She took in a long breath as the car came to a halt around a courtyard, and saw reporters and media persons being pushed behind lines by uniformed constables.

The door opened before her chauffeur had even moved. Expecting Vikram, Zara put on a wide smile and stepped out of the car.

Instead, it was the man who'd always held her heart in the palm of his hand.

Zara's smile fell, and she felt a swooping sensation in her belly—the ache from two months ago just as acute and fresh as if it had been yesterday that he'd left her. A small part of her wanted to get back into the car and drive away. To never see him again.

A large part of her urged her to throw herself at him and demand that he come back to her. That he take her in his arms and kiss her and hold her, only as he could.

Somehow, Zara managed to suppress both of those voices inside her head and gave her hand into his outstretched one. "I was expecting Vikram," she said softly, even as she could hear the pop of a hundred flashes going off in every direction around them. "You know, the man who doesn't keep disappearing from my life for long stretches of time."

She heard the whispered hiss of his indrawn breath, and felt a savage satisfaction. "You know where to hit me to hurt me the most, don't you, *shahzadi*?"

"Do I?" she said fluttering her lashes. To the world, they looked like lovers, with their fingers laced together. Their gazes greedily drinking in each other after a long drought. Zara was sure it was desperation she spied in his eyes. Naked hunger. Raw longing. Because for two months, she'd seen the same emotions in her own eyes when she looked at the mirror, morning, noon or night.

Who the hell was he punishing? she wanted to ask.

"And since you disappeared to God knows where for two months without a word, and it was Vikram who kept an eye on me, it's not that much of a stretch, is it?"

Draping his arm around her shoulders, he subtly adjusted their bodies until he could bend and kiss her cheek. Her skin felt as if it would catch on fire from the simple contact. "I don't begrudge your friendship with him. And he's always been a good brother to me. Even when I was calling him names. He agreed to keep an eye on you, without asking me exactly how I'd mucked up everything."

Her gaze jerked to his. "What?" Zara saw the truth in his eyes. Truth that gave her hope. Hope she suppressed by embracing anger instead. "I don't need you to appoint a keeper to look after me. I'm very capable of looking after myself."

"I have no doubt about that, *shahzadi.* Whatever I did was for my own peace of mind. I had to leave for Switzerland immediately and I couldn't get out of it. Bhai, I knew, you wouldn't refuse."

"I take back everything I said about parenting this baby together. You can't flit in and out of my life whenever you feel like it—"

"I knew I was wrong the moment I left you, Zara. That I was making the biggest mistake of my life."

Zara's heart thundered in her chest. "And it took you two months to say this to me?"

"By the time Bhai found me looking at the bloopers from the movie, like a drunken Devdas raving about his lost lover and I'd recovered from the hangover, I was already late for the flight to Switzerland. And once I was there… I couldn't leave until I finished the postproduction work on my docuseries.

"I only arrived back home a few hours ago. Zara—"

She had no idea what he'd been about to say, because an avalanche of reporters descended on them and Zara forced a smile and walked up the path with him, arm in arm.

The premiere of the biopic showed to rave reviews. Zara and Vikram's performances were off the charts and Virat was being lauded once again as the most brilliant director of their generation. The movie was already being touted as one of those once-in-a-century intersections of commercial and creative storytelling.

It was the biggest night of Virat's life. And yet, it had nothing to do with the movie. In fact, he'd found his attention wandering again and again to the woman sitting next to him in the dark theater, the scent of jasmine in her hair winding through him.

All day, he'd felt jittery. He'd thought he'd calm down once he saw her.

When she'd stepped out of her car, that beautiful silk sari draping perfectly around her growing belly, he'd nearly fallen to his knees. He'd wanted to beg her right there and then for forgiveness. For acting like a thick-skulled fool.

But that wasn't him. What he wanted to share with Zara was private and intimate and bound his very soul to hers. The three hours of the movie, and the two hours on top of that, meeting and greeting critics and reviewers and peers alike, had felt like torture.

And now, with her head lolling around on his shoulder in the moving car, the drive toward his grandparents' old bungalow felt like the longest of his entire life.

Zara came awake slowly when her head lolled onto a hard shoulder. First, she closed her mouth since she knew she must have fallen asleep with it open, like a fish. This falling asleep whenever and wherever was really one of her least favorite things about being pregnant.

This and the feverish dream she'd had that the scent filling her nostrils and lungs was Virat's. It was there now, too—a deliciously familiar cocktail of sandalwood and the cigar he smoked when he was nervous—filling her with that achingly desperate longing.

She fluttered her eyelashes open and found his dark eyes looking into hers. There was that look that she loved—as if she was his past, present and future. The look he gave her only when he made love to her. Or when he thought she wasn't looking.

"You fell asleep in the car."

Zara nodded. "Yeah, I sleep about sixteen hours a day now," she said, just to say something. He was carrying her, she realized, her other senses slowly coming awake.

Carrying her over the threshold of a huge bungalow she'd visited only once. Or twice.

His grandparents' bungalow. And it looked all dressed up. There were strings of lights over the arched entrance and flower garlands hanging everywhere. Strains of *shehnai* came next and Zara fidgeted in his arms. "Put me down, Virat," she barked, feeling as if she was walking through her favorite dream.

Or her worst nightmare, if one looked at it in a certain way.

"Almost there, *shahzadi*," he whispered, and then they were in the inner courtyard where there was a small raised dais in the center. All dressed up with lights and more flowers, like a wedding *mandap*.

And there were people standing around, watching them with curious eyes. Vikram and Naina—with expressions almost like trepidation in their eyes—and Virat's grandmother, with a soft smile, and Anya Raawal next to her. On the other side stood Virat's best friend, AJ, and his wife, Zara's friend Anna. And beaming at her was her mother in front of the *mandap*, with Virat's parents a little distance away. Avidly gazing at both of them.

It was the wedding party she'd planned for. On closer inspection, Zara realized there were exactly the same flowers and music and decorations she'd picked. She looked down at herself and realized it was, of course, the same sari that she and Naina had chosen from a designer's catalog.

Zara's heart might have catapulted out of her chest if Virat hadn't gently brought her down to her feet and enveloped her in his arms. As though shielding her from prying eyes. She felt the tension in him when he embraced her tighter. Almost as if he were a tuning fork vibrating to someone else's frequency.

Hers, she realized slowly.

"Will you marry me, *shahzadi*? Today? Now?" he said and Zara felt as if she might burst into tears.

"Why?" she muttered through a sob half-ready to erupt from her chest.

Virat went on his knees and pressed his face into her belly. When he looked up at her, shock and wonder and so many emotions filled his eyes that Zara had tears in her own. "Because I can't live without you. Because you were always the woman for me. Because I never stopped loving you.

"You were right, Zara. I was a coward. I didn't trust you. And I didn't trust myself, either. I… thought becoming successful in my own right would prove to you and myself that I was enough. But you showed me that I was already enough.

"You bring out the best in me, *shahzadi*. I understand exactly why you felt you had to leave me ten years ago, and even when you did, you still gave me direction in life. Let me show you how much I love you now, Zara. Let me be the father of our child. Let me be the man my Queen deserves."

Zara buried her hands in his hair, tears falling freely onto her cheeks. "Why wait two months to tell me, Virat? Why… I thought you'd really abandoned me. I thought you were punishing me for leaving you ten years ago."

"God, no, Zara. This was about me needing to face up to my own insecurities. My own cowardice. I had a lot to work through…needed to take a long, hard look at myself. I needed to be sure that I would never hurt you like that again. That I wouldn't repeat past mistakes.

"Say yes, Zara. I will spend the rest of our lives showing you how much I love you. How much I deserve you."

When Zara would have flopped onto her knees to join him, he leaped to his feet and held her. "You already have me, Virat. You've always had me."

And then he was kissing her and Zara thought her heart might burst with happiness.

As they walked toward the *mandap*, she tucked her arm through his and leaned close to whisper, "It's a boy," and the joy that filled his eyes was so raw and real that Zara stopped him and stole another kiss.

Whoops and laughter surrounded them as she clung to Virat breathlessly. "What do you think of living here?" he asked then and Zara looked around in surprise.

"But Daadiji lives here," she said, looking at his grandmother.

"Daadi has decided to move back in with Mama and Papa. Since Vikram took the ring that my Daadu gave her, I asked her if we could have this bungalow."

"And?"

He grinned. "She laughed and said she'd been waiting forever for me to ask her. That they'd talked when Daadu had been alive and he wanted me to have the house. She told me it has always been mine.

"It was just waiting for me to claim it."

Zara squeezed his hand and he smiled ruefully. There was a wealth of pain and regret in his eyes but there was a new kind of joy, too. As if he'd released a burden that had claimed him for too long. "Isn't it weird how I always had her and Vikram and Anya and Daadu's love and support, and yet I craved the acceptance of the one man who was too small to give it?"

She nodded. But she knew old wounds didn't heal that easily. That people were wired to want what they didn't have. For months after seeing Saleem's true colors, she'd still gone on believing his empty promises that he would do better next time. That he wouldn't fly into jealous rages and threaten her. That he would control himself better. In the end, Zara had hated his quiet, loving moods even worse than the angry rants that always followed. Because the latter had been the reality of the man. And the former had just filled her full of a poisonous, false hope that crushed her every time he didn't keep his promises.

"Daadu used to call me Choté Raawal Sahib, you know. I forgot about it until Daadi and Vikram reminded me two days ago. I kept them at a distance, too, when all I had to do was to show them how much it hurt. How much I craved to be a part of all this. So many good things I suppressed under bitterness…

"It took you to give me that courage to reach out and ask for what I needed, Zara. It took you to make me see I already had everything I needed. That I was a Raawal where it mattered.

"In my heart."

Zara pressed her face to his chest then, and he held her tight.

"My grandfather built this house for my grandmother," he said, enfolding her in those strong arms. "It represents everything I loved about him, everything he taught me a Raawal man should have—loyalty and kindness and, above all, love. Daadu told me stories, made sagas about love. Because he said it trumps everything else.

"They were married for fifty-seven years, Zara. Can you imagine loving an entire lifetime together like that?"

And there was the romantic man she'd fallen in love with. His heart in his eyes. His love in his words.

Zara simply said yes.

"And the cool shadow of their marriage is what saved Bhai, me and Anya in the end from the toxic heat of our parents' relationship. It taught us how powerful true love can be. I want that kind of marriage, Zara. I want to believe that we will last a hundred years."

There was need and love in those words but Zara realized he was asking her to lend him a little faith, too. And she had it in tons. She had enough to last them a few lifetimes together.

Zara nodded, tears forming a lump in her throat again. She raised his hand to her mouth, kissed the back of it and whispered, "To a hundred years together. To forever."

And then the wedding party took over, pulling her away from her groom, and Zara blew him a kiss, knowing this time their separation would only last a few minutes.

Because forever was waiting for them.

* * * * *

Blown away by The Surprise Bollywood Baby?
Make sure you don't miss the first installment in the Born into Bollywood duet

Claiming His Bollywood Cinderella

Why not also have a look at these other stories by Tara Pammi?

Sicilian's Bride for a Price
An Innocent to Tame the Italian
A Deal to Carry the Italian's Heir
The Flaw in His Marriage Plan

All available now

COMING NEXT MONTH FROM

HARLEQUIN

PRESENTS

Available March 30, 2021

#3897 THE SECRET THAT CAN'T BE HIDDEN

Rich, Ruthless & Greek

by Caitlin Crews

Kendra Connolly has never forgotten her fleeting first encounter with billionaire Balthazar Skalas. When they're reunited, she gives in to temptation—completely. It's a decision made in the heat of the moment that will change her life forever...

#3898 CINDERELLA IN THE BOSS'S PALAZZO

by Julia James

Haunted by his past, wealthy Italian Evandro has sworn off romance—but he can't ignore the chemistry with his daughter's fiery new tutor, Jenna. The pair may clash, but their attraction is ready to hit boiling point...

#3899 THE GREEK WEDDING SHE NEVER HAD

Innocent Summer Brides

by Chantelle Shaw

Eleanor broke off her engagement to devastatingly handsome tycoon Jace, believing he only wanted her family's business. Now to save it, she must accept his second proposal! And shockingly, their chemistry has lost none of its heat...

#3900 WAYS TO RUIN A ROYAL REPUTATION

Signed, Sealed...Seduced

by Dani Collins

King Luca never craved the throne, but to abdicate, he must become a royal disgrace! He'll need Amy Miller's PR genius to fan the flames of scandal, but passionate flames may just ignite in the process...

HPCNMRA0321

#3901 BRIDE BEHIND THE DESERT VEIL

The Marchetti Dynasty

by Abby Green

After surrendering to passion with a mystery woman, Sharif Marchetti must erase their desert encounter from his memory. Until they meet again...as he lifts the veil of his convenient wife!

#3902 THE ITALIAN'S FORBIDDEN VIRGIN

Those Notorious Romanos

by Carol Marinelli

Italian tycoon Gian de Luca knows Ariana Romano is off-limits. She's his mentor's daughter, and her drama queen reputation precedes her. But when he offers her comfort one night, he's shocked to discover she's a virgin. Perhaps he's been wrong about her all along...

#3903 HIS STOLEN INNOCENT'S VOW

The Queen's Guard

by Marcella Bell

For billionaire Drake Andros, only marriage and an heir from Helene d'Tierrza will recover what was stolen from him. Their chemistry may persuade her to help him, but her vow of innocence may complicate his plan...

#3904 ONE HOT NEW YORK NIGHT

Wanted: A Billionaire

by Melanie Milburne

A sizzling night of passion is exactly what Zoey Brackenfield needs. And since it's with Finn O'Connell, business rival and notorious playboy, there's zero chance of heartbreak. That is, until she starts craving his exhilarating touch...

SPECIAL EXCERPT FROM

HARLEQUIN
PRESENTS

For billionaire Drake Andros, only marriage and an heir from Helene d'Tierrza will recover what was stolen from him. Their chemistry may persuade her to help him, but her vow of innocence may complicate his plan…

Read on for a sneak preview of Marcella Bell's next story for Harlequin Presents His Stolen Innocent's Vow.

"I can't," she repeated, her voice low and earnest. "I can't, because when I went to him as he lay dying, I looked him in his eyes and swore to him that the d'Tierrza line would end with me, that there would be no d'Tierrza children to inherit the lands or title and that I would see to it that the family name was wiped from the face of the earth so that everything he had ever worked for, or cared about, was lost to history, the legacy he cared so much about nothing but dust. I swore to him that I would never marry and never have children, that not a trace of his legacy would be left on this planet."

For a moment, there was a pause, as if the room itself had sucked in a hiss of irritation. The muscles in his neck tensed, then flexed, though he remained otherwise motionless. He blinked as if in slow motion, the movement a sigh, carrying something much deeper than frustration, though no sound came out. Hel's chest squeezed as she merely observed him. She felt like she'd let him down in some monumental way, though they'd only just become reacquainted. She struggled to understand why the sensation was so familiar until she recognized the experience of being in the presence of her father.

Then he opened his eyes again, and instead of the cold green disdain her heart expected, they still burned that fascinating warm brown—a heat that was a steady home fire, as comforting as the imaginary family she'd dreamed up as a child—and all of the taut disappointment in the air was gone.

Her vow was a hiccup in his plans. That he had a low tolerance for hiccups was becoming clear. How she knew any of this when he had revealed so little in his reaction, and her mind only now offered up hazy memories of him as a young man, she didn't know.

She offered a shrug and an airy laugh in consolation, mildly embarrassed about the whole thing though she was simultaneously unsure as to exactly why. "Otherwise, you know, I'd be all in. Despite the whole abduction…" Her cheeks were hot, likely bright pink, but it couldn't be helped, so she made the joke anyway, despite the risk that it might bring his eyes to her face, that it might mean their gazes locked again and he stole her breath again.

Of course, that was what happened. And then there was that smile again, the one that said he knew all about the strange, mesmerizing power he had over her, and it pleased him.

Whether he was the kind of man who used his power for good or evil had yet to be determined.

Either way, beneath that infuriating smile, deep in his endless brown eyes, was the sharp attunement of a predator locked on its target. "Give me a week." His face may not have changed, but his voice gave him away, a trace of hoarseness, as if his sails had been slashed and the wind slipped through them, threaded it, a strange hint of something Hel might have described as desperation…if it had come from anyone other than him.

"What?" she asked.

"Give me a week to change your mind."